I0551685

Aiding Revenge

Jodi Clark

AUTHOR'S NOTE: This story is a work of fiction. Names, characters, places and incidents are a product of the author's imagination and any resemblance to actual persons, places or events are entirely coincidental.

United States Copyright © 2013 Jodi Clark
Published by Lulu

ISBN 978-0-9891207-0-8

All rights reserved. No portion of this book may be reproduced, stored in a retrieval system or transmitted in any form or by any means without written permission by the author.

Chapter 1

The undersized and oppressive office bustled with a long rectangular table of aged volunteers, industriously stuffing envelopes with campaign flyers for Governor Don Tatum's re-election. During his term, he had proven himself a motivated and highly regarded servant for the residents in his home state of Indiana. A man of his word, he had worked to amend laws, cleaned up distressed neighborhoods, and created jobs for the unemployed. The Governor was a well-respected family man and pillar of the community who carried himself with immeasurable class and flair everywhere that he went. With a promising career, his attorney wife of sophistication and intellect, and two seemingly wholesome children, Don Tatum was the epitome of excellence.

A small group sat in one corner of the office, on the phones raising campaign donations, when Shana Bradley breezed in. The young, auburn-haired beauty, pristinely clad in her red silk blouse, controlled the room from the moment that she entered. Effortlessly, she captured the attention of the wide-eyed males while the women enviously admired her physical perfection.

"Hello," the campaign leader, Donna, greeted with a wary smile and an extended hand, "you must be Shana."

"Hi, yes, we spoke on the phone yesterday," Shana returned the expression with a handshake and her addictive smile. "I'm here to volunteer for the Governor's campaign."

"Well, we certainly appreciate the help." The older woman directed her new subordinate to sit with them. "We are just mailing out these flyers," She said, handing her a heap.

Shana gazed at the photo of the handsome and distinguished dark-haired man in his black suit with ocean eyes and an esteemed smile. Don Tatum's image captured her admiration as she yearned to know him. In her eyes, he was a heroic knight, a man of unblemished quality.

"How long have you been a supporter of the Governor?" One of the women probed.

"Oh, I've been an advocate of his during his entire political career," the young woman suavely answered with an intellectual smile. "He has done amazing things for the community and I think that he's a remarkable leader and role model." What she really wanted to say that he was the man she

2

dreamed of, the one she adored and yearned to spend her life with.

"He is a great man," the room's occupants agreed as they steadily continued their campaign efforts.

"Does he stop in here often?" Shana attempted her question in a casual tone, though desperate to meet him. She had been to nearly all of his public events, eagerly awaiting the opportunity to be noticed by him, all to no avail, but this, she felt, was her chance at a successful encounter.

"Yes, with this being his campaign headquarters, we actually see him quite frequently," another volunteer answered. "In fact, there is a dinner for all of us this weekend if you'd like to attend. It's kind of a strategy meeting and appreciation dinner combined."

"Sounds great," Shana beamed. Of course she would attend the function, especially since the Governor would be there. She couldn't wait to be relieved of her duty at his campaign headquarters so that she could begin her search for the perfect dress, the one that would take his breath away. If she was finally going to meet Don Tatum, there was extensive preparation involved. She had to be flawless to capture his intrigue.

In the few hours that ensued, Shana listened to the chatter among the volunteers and occasionally, she tried to include herself but she had no real interest in making friends. She was there for only one reason, to connect with her soul mate.

That evening, Shana made a swift escape to find the ideal dress. The dinner was in just two days and there was much to be done. As she breezed through one store after another, she assessed gowns of satin, velvet and silk and conservative cocktail dresses, but none appeared noble enough for the occasion. She needed a show-stopper, an ensemble of a sexy elegance and sophistication. At her final destination, she spotted the crimson, semi-revealing splendor, a floor length, flowy gown that hugged her body with a deep slit up the back that left little to the imagination. It was magnificent and perfect for the lasting impression that she was hoping to make on the Governor.

"Your total comes to seven hundred fifty dollars," the pretentious clerk informed as if it was fifty cents. The price of the dress was Shana's entire savings but it was well worth the money if it grabbed Don Tatum's attention.

With the perfect dress arose the need for the precise accessories which she found the following day, on her way home from the campaign headquarters. In her apartment that night, Shana put on the complete ensemble and stared proudly into her full length mirror, delighted at her stunning image.

"If this doesn't get his attention, nothing will," she told her reflection while revealing enough cleavage to capture the eye of any man. As she primped, she imagined herself on the arm of the Governor. "Hello, I'm Mrs. Tatum," she grinned in the mirror. With the flyer photo of him cut out and taped to the wall next to it, she stood valiantly, rehearsing her words and demeanor for her meeting with him, over and over again, until she found perfection. Every detail had to be meticulous and his impression of her needed to be extraordinary. Her only obstacle, she thought, was his wife, Felicia. "When Don sees me, he won't even remember who she is." Shana smirked between poses. She was thrilled at the opportunity to finally meet the man of her dreams and she felt that once he noticed her, the possibilities would be endless. All that she needed to do was be seen by him. The rest would surely take care of itself.

After what felt to her like a lifetime of waiting, Saturday finally arrived, and Shana greeted her beautician friend, Carla, who had arrived at her house to refine her hair for the campaign dinner that evening.

"Tonight is the big night," her friend commented as she laid out her styling supplies.

"Yes, and I am so excited!" Shana replied ecstatically. "I'm so anxious to finally meet Don."

"You refer to him like you already know each other," the stylist joked, but it was always what Shana referred to him as when she spoke of him.

"I feel like we do already know each other. I mean, I know everything that there is about him."

"Well, try not to be too forward. You don't want him to think that you're obsessed or something." Her friend began putting coils into her auburn hair to be swept up into a classy updo.

"I'm not obsessed. I'm confident. He's in for the whirlwind of his life," she responded with a devious grin, eager to capture his attention. Carla shook her head with a snicker.

5

"How are you going to get his attention?" Her friend asked. "Do you know how many people will probably be there?"

"Yes, but have you seen me in this dress?"

"You are crazy, girl." Carla replied with a giggle.

"Crazy in love," Shana told her. Though they had never before met, her heart told her that she and the Governor were soul mates and she was convinced that they were meant for each other. He was everything that she had ever wanted in a man. "I just have to figure out what I'm going to say to him when I finally do get his attention."

"How about something like, 'Meet the new Mrs. Tatum.'" The hair stylist suggested and the pair laughed. Shana stared in the mirror, envisioning herself in a white wedding gown, sashaying down the aisle to be Don Tatum's wife, the Governor's wife. It was her dream. She pictured herself having dinner ready, each night, when he came home and snuggling together on the sofa as he read the newspaper or watched television. She dreamed of what it would be like to make love to the man that she had craved for so long.

At thirty three years old, Shana had certainly had her share of boyfriends, the quarterback of the high school football team who she had caught with another cheerleader, the studious boy in a couple of her classes who she had spotted eyeing her while she did her assignments, the fraternity president in college, who was more into himself and partying than her. None of them had been esteemed enough for her exquisite taste in a gentleman. It would take someone extraordinary who had substance and intellect, a man with influence and the respect of those around him. The boys that she had dated up to that point simply didn't qualify for her long list of requirements. Shana realized that she needed someone who could meet her high standards and treasured her the way that she felt she deserved. Very few men had been able to meet her criteria, but she viewed Governor Tatum as the ideal candidate. He met her every requirement and more, and she knew that he was meant for her. There was no other man that could compare to the attributes that Don Tatum held. From the first moment that she had seen him on television, just after his election, she knew that she needed to have him. He was her muse and the man that she measured every other one against. She recognized his family values, observing the way that he smiled at his wife and took pride in his children in the media, and she saw how well respected he was by his colleagues and peers. Shana viewed Don Tatum as the perfect man, flawless in his essence and the only suitable husband for her.

"I realize he has a wife but it's me he belongs with," she told her friend. "I do feel for his wife, but he and I can take care of the children while she gets visitations. It isn't ideal but people make it work."

Carla listened as her friend strategically planned her future with the governor with real belief in it becoming a reality. She could see Shana's unhealthy obsession with him and had tried to reason with her but it was to no avail. She recalled her similar obsessions with a handful of other guys in her high school and college years, all who seemed incapable of having an adequate relationship and had taken advantage of her. Even still, Shana had pledged her unwavering love to each and every one of them until the next one came along. Carla had watched her self-destruct when it came to men with each breakup adding to her lack of self-esteem. She had made attempts in the past to talk to her friend about falling too hard too fast for the men she wanted but Shana was never willing to hear it and she could never seem to break the pattern.

Shana arrived at the hotel restaurant early, eloquently attired in her strapless dress and long tresses, draped like silk, over her tanned shoulders. Her diamond studded necklace and earrings complimented her ensemble with utter perfection. She felt magnificent and she anxiously anticipated the Governor's reaction to his sight of her. Surely, she would sweep him off his feet, she thought.

A dining room of seventy suited men and superbly dressed women housed tables of candlelight and fine china as the elegance of soft piano music graced the background. Shana glanced around the sea of strangers, hoping to stand out among them. She was determined to win the Governor's interest.

"Hello," a distinguished, silver haired man greeted after pulling a chair out for his supercilious wife, who gave an immediate snub to Shana. "I'm Peter Fallon and this is my wife, Darlene. Do you mind if we share your table?"

"Oh, no, not at all," she replied with a smile. "I'm Shana Bradley. I work on Governor Tatum's campaign team, along with being his most loyal supporter."

"Nice to meet you, Shana," he said. "I'm an aide in his office." Her eyes widened with amazement at her luck to be seated with someone with such close ties to Don Tatum.

"Really?" She replied with fascination. "Tell me, what is he like?"

"Oh, well," he stammered, "he's just like what you see on television, distinguished and respectable, someone who truly cares about Indiana's needs. He's a good man."

"I knew it!" She told herself. "I would love to meet him," Shana responded in a somewhat seductive tone, hinting for an introduction through her new acquaintance. Without hesitation, Peter, exceedingly intrigued with her good looks, offered to introduce her to the Governor later in the evening, and she was delighted.

"Good evening, ladies and gentlemen," a man spoke from the podium. "Thank you all for coming out tonight in honor of our Governor and this great state of Indiana. Without further ado, please welcome Governor Donald Tatum."

The restaurant erupted in applause as he took his place at the microphone, and Shana relished the view. He looked even more handsome in person, she thought, with his dark hair that barely swept the back of his collar, his physique in the tailored gray suit and the strong jaw line of his rugged face.

"Good evening, everyone," he began. "I would first like to thank you all for joining my family and me this evening," he stated. "I truly appreciate all of your dedication and efforts." As he spoke, she stared hungrily at him, fantasizing about being his lover and his wife, savoring his good looks, his deep voice and his contagious, inviting smile. She had just been promised an introduction and she planned to make the best of it with an unforgettable impression on the Governor. Political status aside, he was still a man and she was an expert at holding their attention. It was an art that she had easily perfected.

Shana noticed Peter's constant glances and exerted efforts to make conversation with her while his agitated wife worked to divert his attention. After dinner and two glasses of wine, Shana was eager to meet the governor. The Fallons had taken to the dance floor twenty minutes prior and still hadn't returned, and Shana's frustration festered. She needed to meet Don Tatum before he left the event, which appeared to be at any moment. She needed to make her move as soon as possible. He was hardly approachable with the mob that encased him, each awaiting his opportunity to speak to him. Shana edged her way through the crowd with determination, squeezing herself between people and even butting in front of them until finally, she stood before him. With her best smile, she introduced herself with a handshake.

"I am, by far, your biggest supporter," she began with a sparkle in her eye and, like a child meeting its idol, her heart raced with enthusiasm.

Already, she wondered what he thought of her, but he didn't display the same captivation that she was used to seeing on men that she met.

"Well, thank you," he replied with an enlightened grin. "It's a pleasure to meet you." She needed more from him.

"As a matter of fact, I recently began working on your campaign, at the headquarters." She could feel the nudges on her sides and back of those trying to get their greetings in.

"That's wonderful and very much appreciated," he responded warmly but there was nothing that seemed to distinguish her from the rest of his admirers. Her conversation was interrupted by another bystander who gave an impolite shove to get her introduction in. When it was apparent that her time with the Governor was done, Shana crossly made her way back to her seat. Her conversation with him wasn't as she had imagined. She hadn't had the time to leave the lasting impression that she was aiming for and, in fact, he seemed to have hardly even noticed her.

"So, you spoke to Governor Tatum, I see," Peter Fallon remarked with an inebriated smile.

"Oh, now you come off of the dance floor!" Shana thought to herself. Where was he when she needed him? With as much politeness as she could muster, she nodded. "I was only able to speak with him for a second. He's quite popular." With a glance around the room, she spotted the Governor's socialite wife working the room with handshakes and hugs. "Ugh!" Shana said to herself, wondering what that woman had that she didn't. Felicia was charismatic and sophisticated with her animated grin and tall stature but she was far from the classic beauty that she imagined Don being with. Her blond hair was swept up into flowing curls as she worked the room in shimmering, silver lace that matched her husband. Shana made her exit, vowing to reconnect with Don Tatum when he visited his campaign headquarters.

She lay in bed, that night, reliving their introduction in her mind and searching for things that she could have done differently to make more of an impression. As the image of his larger than life spouse invaded her thoughts, she envisioned herself in her place, socializing at various events and galas and nestled in bed with Don each night, breathing in his aura. She wondered if the couple had a happy marriage but hoped it had grown stale and bitter so that he would be easily seduced by her. The notion of him with another woman suffocated her. She was convinced that she appreciated him far more than his wife did. All she needed was the opportunity to prove it to him. Deep within her soul, she was had no doubt that they were meant for each other and she pledged to be with him, no matter what the cost.

Chapter 2

The few days that followed at the Governor's campaign headquarters were hectic, stuffing envelopes and making one phone call after another for vows of support and financial donations. Shana dressed in her finest ensembles each day, hoping for his appearance. She wanted to be prepared to make her finest impression on him at any moment.

It was clear to her that she wasn't favored by many of the female campaign staff. Their pretentious efforts of small talk with her were frequently overshadowed by their stares out of the corner of her eye, and she had overheard their gossip about her on several occasions.

"She thinks she's really something," they said or "she seems very uppity." Someone, it seemed, always had a comment about her as if they were experts on her character. Though she couldn't deny that their criticisms troubled her, she reminded herself that she wasn't there to make friends. Her entire purpose for being there was to snag Don Tatum and, once she did, she would ensure that each of them ate their callous words. Most of the men on the team had a very different opinion about Shana, rapt in her magnetism. She frequently caught their ogles and a few, even two that were married, had already been courageous enough to ask her out, though she had politely declined every invitation. She had eyes for only one man and she was willing to wait for him.

Shana was taken by surprise the following week when finally, the Governor made a surprise appearance at the headquarters. The mere sight of him, handsomely dressed in his newly pressed, pinstriped suit and dark, layered hair stole her focus, causing her to hang up the phone on one of the state's residents that she had been speaking to.

"Hello everyone," he greeted with a wave and smile of gratitude, and her heart raced with anticipation of meeting him. He began to circulate himself to each section of the long rectangular table, chatting with his supporters. "You are all doing great work," Shana heard him say. "I really appreciate it." She stared, awestruck by him, hardly able to wait the time that it was taking him to make his way toward her, in the back of the room. In her mind, she rehearsed the words that she would say to him. It had to be something brilliant that would retain his attention and make him want to see her again. It had to be intellectual conversation for a man so esteemed.

Governor Tatum chatted his way to the back of the room after some time and with an extended hand, he kindly greeted Shana.

"We met at the dinner a couple of weeks ago," she reminded him and, in her most seductive eyes and voice, she added, "I'm your biggest supporter, remember?" Intellect had abruptly and unintentionally been replaced by sex appeal. It was what she knew best. With a hint of confusion in his face, seemingly searching his memory for their prior introduction, he smiled with a nod.

"I appreciate your hard work on this campaign," the Governor kindly remarked before continuing his round of handshakes and gratitude.

"That's it?" Shana said to herself with disappointment. Don Tatum had barely spoken to her. She hadn't stood above the crowd like she assumed that she would. He had treated her just as he did everyone else at his headquarters and she was incensed over his neglect. "I have the constant attention of every man in this room and he hardly noticed me?" She couldn't understand why she was unable to gain his interest and his actions appalled her.

In her apartment that evening, as their brief conversation repeatedly replayed in her mind, Shana pondered what went wrong. Why hadn't she grabbed his attention? There wasn't a man in town that didn't glue their eyes to her so how could Don not have taken notice? It made no sense to her. Even the Governor's loyally married aide, Peter

Fallon, had slipped her his card on her way out the door at the appreciation dinner.

"I guess I'm just going to have to up my game," Shana told herself with a fresh idea.

The next day, Shana found her most well-fitting business suit and applied her makeup with flawless precision. The curled ends of her long, auburn hair danced gently across her shoulders as she grabbed her envelope and headed for the Governor's office.

"Hello, I'm Shana Bradley, a staff member of Governor Tatum's campaign team," she told the receptionist in her most professional tone. "I'm here to see Peter Fallon."

The middle aged receptionist, suspiciously eyeing the vixen, asked if she had an appointment. She knew that, as soon as Peter realized who she was, she wouldn't need one.

"No, actually, I don't. I was asked to bring these campaign flyers to him. I presume that time is of the essence," she fibbed.

"One moment please," the woman responded while dialing the aide's extension. "Mr. Fallon, there is a Ms. Bradley here to see you. She says that she has some campaign flyers for you." After their conversation, the receptionist glared at her. "You can just leave the flyers with me and I'll see that Mr. Fallon gets them." Shana wasn't going to be dismissed that easily.

"Well, ordinarily I would, ma'am, but you see, these are for Mr. Fallon's approval and I have some revision options to discuss with him. As I mentioned, time is of the essence," Shana replied with an innocent smile. "It will only take a few minutes of his time so could you please try again?" Within a few minutes, an exasperated Peter appeared in the lobby and the vision of her immediately restored his fascination.

"Ms. Bradley, hello," he greeted as he approached to shake her hand. Her seductive smile intrigued him enough to be invited into his office. "Please, sit down," he offered as he descended with an arrogant grin into his black leather chair. "To what do I owe this extreme pleasure?" The undersized, balding man asked with a flirtatious overtone. He sickened her with his perverted approach. She loathed the kind of man he was, assuming that his wealth and status could acquire whatever he wanted, including her.

"Well," Shana began, slowly crossing one knee over the other while Peter gawked with hunger, "I created some new campaign material for Governor Tatum, but I thought I would get your opinion on them first," she said in her most alluring voice. "I mean, you're obviously a brilliant man, and I feel that your input would be extremely beneficial." She took three different flyer designs from the envelope and slowly bent over Peter's desk, intentionally revealing her partially exposed cleavage to him. His eyes fell rapidly, in awe, as he licked his lips. "What do you think?" The seductress asked him artfully.

She heard him gulp as he stammered through his response. "Oh, well, um, well, I think they're fantastic."

Shana peered into his eyes as if she craved him. "Are we still talking about the flyers?" She asked, boasting a smile.

"Oh, well, that depends, I suppose," Peter said, seemingly unconfident of his next move.

"You see, Mr. Fallon . . ."

"Please, call me Peter," he jubilantly intervened.

She openly glanced down at his manhood and with a leer, back up at him. "Peter. You see, I have been striving for so many years to work with the Governor and well, I thought that if I could impress him with my . . ." she paused as he focused on her crimson lips, ". . . flyers, then maybe he would grant me the opportunity." Shana could see her allure winning over the Governor's aide. "I'm very experienced and always willing to try new things," she added with a smile. Peter was practically salivating when he agreed to help Shana. She had him exactly where she wanted him.

"Why don't we discuss this further over dinner tonight," he suggested, loosening his tie as his forehead glistened.

"That sounds fantastic but I was hoping to show the flyers to Governor Tatum while I'm here." Peter informed Shana that Don was out of town for a few days, campaigning while still reiterating his dinner invitation in a manner that insisted he was her only route to the governor.

"I'll see you tonight," she smiled with a sexy stroll to the door as he watched with glory on his face.

That evening, the pair was seated near an exquisite stone fireplace in a lavish restaurant, uptown. As soft piano music played in the background, Peter sat, admiring Shana in her emerald satin dress which left little to the imagination. She was nauseated by his parody but it was her only way of getting closer to the Governor. Her beauty was her secret weapon and she had to play the game.

"You look amazing," Peter complimented as she sipped her red wine with the candlelight setting her tanned skin aglow, her eyes beckoning him.

"Why don't we just cut to the chase," Shana told him. "We're adults and I think you and I both know where this is going. I want to work closely with Governor Tatum and you are able to help me with that, so you benefit me and I'll do the same for you, okay?" She spoke tenderly in a tone that made it impossible to refuse.

They made a swift exit to her apartment after dinner. She saw no reason to continue the cat and mouse game when both were well aware of what they were after. She was anything but attracted to Peter, making her task grueling, but she had to make him think otherwise.

"I'm not happy with my wife," he moaned as she kissed his neck, unbuttoning his striped dress shirt. Her touch radiated him as if he had never before experienced a woman and she imagined him as Don.

Shana was revolted by her erroneous seduction, and her skin crawled at his touch. She was grateful to have had several glasses of wine to assist her through it. Still, in her mind, it was a small price to pay for the Governor's attention. Peter savored every part of her, slowly working his way around his playground as he panted heavily with ecstasy.

"You are so sexy." She swore that he was drooling on her but hoped it was a sign that the tryst would be quick.

"Just hurry up!" She thought to herself, already eager to forget the experience. He seemed to be taking his time with her and she was growing increasingly irritated. She wasn't interested in making it an all night event, but it seemed apparent that he was in no rush to reach his goal.

After two agonizing hours of faking her way through the sexual encounter, she was more than ready for him to leave her apartment.

"You were incredible, baby," he complimented in an attempted alluring, superior tone while zipping his pants with a beaming grin.

"So, I got the job?" She needed to seal their deal.

"You got it," he said. "Be there bright and early on Monday morning."

"Great!"

"Oh," Peter said returning from his way out the door, "and I can't wait to get together again." He left her with a kiss on the neck. She forced a gracious smile.

"That won't be happening," Shana thought. Seeing him again wasn't part of their deal. She hurried to a scalding shower in an attempt to wash him off of her. She felt as if a snake had just crawled all over her body and she couldn't seem to get clean enough. "Thank God that's over!" She told herself.

Shana arose early on Monday morning, eager to begin her new job in the Governor's office. She chose a tight-fitting, gray business suit and black heels. Her hair stylishly swept up in a bun, she carefully applied her makeup and caught one final glance in her full-length mirror.

"Hello, this is my first day," she gleefully informed the receptionist who had previously snubbed her the week before. "I'm the new aide to Governor Tatum."

The condescending, middle-aged receptionist let out a snicker and led the new employee back to an empty desk, just outside of Peter's office. "This will be your workstation," she told her.

"Oh, just great," she thought to herself, dissatisfied that she would be working near Peter, whom she didn't care to see again. A few minutes later, he appeared with a smirk.

"Shana, good morning. I'm glad you made it," he greeted with a wink.

"Shouldn't my desk be a little closer to Governor Tatum's if I'm going to be working as his aide?"

"Well, actually, you'll be working as my aide," he corrected. Fury kidnapped her euphoria. It was never mentioned in their deal that she would be working for Peter, and she felt that this was another part of his arrogant game of supremacy.

"May I please talk to you in your office?" She asked him, struggling to maintain her integrity. Shana closed the door and glared at him with outrage. "I'm supposed to be working with the Governor. That was our deal, remember?"

"No, I don't remember that," Peter told her smugly. "I said that you would be an aide in his office, not necessarily for him." With ferocity, she stood, nearly speechless at his treachery. "You can't just walk in as an aide to the Governor but you can earn the position, in time."

Shana was infuriated. Sleeping with Peter was hardly worth being his secretary. Had she known this to be the outcome, she would have rethought her actions. He had slyly fooled her into getting what he wanted when, all the while, she thought that she was calling the shots. Still, she was, at least, working in Don Tatum's office, where she could make herself familiar to him. She felt that if she could befriend him, he would see all that she could offer and she would undoubtedly be promoted to his aide. Until then, she would just have to deal with Peter Fallon.

"It needs to be said that our relationship has to remain private and completely outside of this office," he told her. "I hold an important position here and it would be detrimental to have it leaked out. When we're here, it's strictly business."

"Is he serious?" She had to ask herself. The last thing that she wanted was for anyone to know about their sexual encounter. He spoke, pompously, as if they had begun a new relationship. "Don't worry," she told him. "I assure you that it's just between us."

Shana's monotonous day consisted of answering the phone and typing letters, with frequent glances for the sight of Don who was not to be found. As five o'clock dredged near, Peter summoned his new assistant into his sanctuary.

"How about dinner tonight?" He asked with perversion already gleaming in his face. "I could use a replay of the other night." Shana had no intention of repeating her actions that night.

"I'm sorry but I already have commitments," she politely declined with a blatant lie that she almost felt good about. "Besides, I thought it was clear that it was a one-time thing."

"I see," he responded with an expression of displeasure. "Well, I don't remember that and, since I can relieve you of this job as quickly as I hired you, maybe tomorrow night would be good?" It was painfully obvious to her that Peter wasn't going to give up, and his ego was fed by the power that he held over her.

"This is kind of a hectic week for me, so . . ."

"Shana," he responded with a casual lean against his oak desk and his hand on his chin, "if you intend to maintain a position here, and especially aim for a promotion, you're going to have to acquiesce to my requests as your supervisor."

"You bastard!" She wanted to yell out to him. "How dare you blackmail me into your demented fantasy!" She was the one in control and

23

she refused to relinquish it to him, even if he was her boss. Shana flashed him a stare of distaste before storming out of his office.

That evening, in her apartment, she poured a glass of red wine to soothe her anger. Pacing the maple floor of her living room, she fumed. "I am the one in control here," she assured herself. "I will call the shots, not that perverted scumbag." Shana plopped down on her modest, tan-hued sofa with a sigh of frustration. With her wine glass held up to her eyes, she stared at the crimson contents. "This could be your blood, Mr. Fallon," she remarked with malevolence in her statement. "No one will stand in the way of my relationship with Don." She always spoke of the Governor as though she already knew him and, in her mind, the two were personally involved. Don Tatum was her aspiration, her goal in life. Her world had become absorbed with conquering him, convinced that they were meant to be together.

Chapter 3

The following morning, sipping coffee in front of her computer, Shana opened an email from Governor Tatum's assistant.

Dear Ms. Bradley,
It is with great pleasure that I welcome you to our family as the newest staff member. Your hard work and dedication is sincerely appreciated by all. I hope that this will be a journey of inspiration, insight and, moreover, a rewarding pathway to your own success.

Sincerely Yours,
Governor Don Tatum

The Governor's memo filled her with a euphoric bliss. Though it was a standard letter to all of his new employees, Shana felt that it was written specifically for her. It was a kind sentiment from her soul mate and the beginning of an enduring relationship between them.

"Shana, could you come in here, please?" Peter Fallon's voice was the equivalent to nails on a chalkboard, swords into her spine. She couldn't allow his antics to ruin her good mood. "My wife has her yoga class tonight and I was thinking that we could get together." She was growing increasingly exhausted with excuses not to see him.

"Tonight just isn't good for me, Peter," she fibbed. "I'm not feeling well today. I think I'm coming down with something." Shana hoped that he would accept her response without a rebuttal but his glare warned otherwise. "I promise we'll get together again soon, okay?"

"Kiss me," he casually commanded, needing his assistant to replenish his confidence in her.

"I don't think that's a good idea," she responded with reluctance. "We're in your office. Someone might see us." She struggled to conjure up an excuse. "We have to keep it strictly business here, remember?"

"Yes, you're right," he agreed. "Promise me that we can spend a little time together this week." Shana was willing to say nearly anything that would give her a fast escape from his office so she nodded with compliance.

With her plot not panning out the way that she had hoped, Shana needed a new plan, one that would work quickly to both get her close to the Governor and away from Peter Fallon, who was constantly slithering around her. Since she hadn't yet caught even a sight of Don, she felt that she needed to befriend those who were close to him. His assistant, she thought, was a good place to start. Conjuring up her friendliest smile, Shana found her way to his assistant's desk.

"Hi, I'm Shana Bradley, Peter Fallon's new assistant," she introduced herself to the gray-haired woman. "Since I just started working here, I don't really know anyone yet, so I wondered if you would like to have lunch today?"

"Oh, um, okay," the woman reluctantly answered with bewilderment on her face. "I'm Betty Carlisle."

"It's very nice to meet you, Betty," Shana replied with a gentle handshake. The women sat in a small café uptown, getting to know one another.

"Thank you for inviting me to lunch," Betty said.

"It's my pleasure, and thank you for accepting. It gets a little lonely in the office without anyone to talk to." Shana needed to say all of the things that Don's assistant wanted to hear if she was going to earn her trust. "It must be inspiring to work so closely with Governor Tatum."

"Oh yes, he's a truly wonderful man," Betty responded. "It's really a pleasure for me, and I'm almost sad about retiring next year," she giggled.

"Retiring?" The bells screamed in Shana's ears. She had to find a way to take Betty's position when she retired. It was the perfect opportunity for her. "I am the Governor's biggest supporter. I think that he does great things for the people here, in

27

Indiana. In fact, before I started working in his office, I was on his campaign team. It was very rewarding, but even with all of that, I still haven't had the pleasure of meeting him yet." It was a little white lie that she viewed as harmless.

"Oh, well, I can certainly introduce you," Betty offered. She was playing right into Shana's hands, just as she had hoped. "I suppose that if you are working for him, you should know him, right? Besides, he loves meeting new people and especially new employees."

"Definitely," she snickered. "Betty, thank you so much for being my friend. You are a great lady."

"Oh, no," the aging woman modestly shrugged off her compliment.

"I hope that we can do this more often," Shana told her. Her plan had worked like a charm. Betty had fallen into her hands, perfectly, and she almost felt bad for using her the way that she had to.

Back at the office, Peter awaited her.

"Ugh!" She thought. The mere sight of him repelled her.

"Did you have a good lunch?" He asked her.

"Yes, thanks," she responded, attempting to appear too busy to chat with him.

"Maybe tomorrow, you and I can take a long lunch, huh?" He slyly suggested with a wink and Shana was nauseated at the thought.

"Maybe, we'll see," she responded without even a glance at him.

"No excuses," he told her with a serious voice before returning to his office.

"What have I gotten myself into?" She wondered with a sigh of frustration. Peter Fallon had become an enormous problem for Shana, and she needed a prompt resolution. He was an obstacle that needed to be removed. His constant blackmail and harassment lent cause for her to devise a way to expel him from her life for good, but it couldn't be accomplished while she worked for him, and Betty wouldn't be retiring until the following year. Shana needed to speed up the process. Having her new friend's job would solve her problems and draw her closer to her goal.

Shana dreaded going to the office the next day. She was tangled into a web of deceit that seemed nearly impossible to escape. Peter expected to have an extended lunch with her, which she knew meant another sexual encounter, and she was willing to do almost anything to get out of it. Still, if she wanted to keep her job in the Governor's office, her compliance was imperative. She was out of excuses and there was no other choice but to oblige.

"I'm looking forward to lunch today," her boss said with a devilish wink, in passing, that morning. Shana shook her head in disgust. It was Friday, and her first week at her new job had been agony for her.

Don Tatum hadn't been in the office all week, and she hoped that he would return on Monday. How could she get to know him if he was never around? Her time was limited, forcing the realization that she needed to be aggressive when she finally did see him. Shana typed an email to her new friend.

Good morning, Betty,

I have come up with a few new campaign ideas for Governor Tatum that I'd like to present to him. Will he be in the office next week?

Only a few minutes later, Betty's response sounded on Shana's computer.

Good morning,

The Governor is due back in his office on Monday morning. Have a great weekend!

She was thrilled with Betty's news. Monday was the day that she had to make things happen.

Noon arrived all too soon, and Peter eagerly made his way to his assistant's desk with a jubilant skip in his step. They found a diner close by for lunch, where Shana ate as slowly as she could, trying to buy some extra time. The thought of what was to follow made choking down her food nearly impossible. Nausea was already settling in.

"I've been waiting all week for this," Peter told her. "Watching you in the office sets me on fire." He smirked with excitement, and she loathed how his lewdness thrilled him. "I can't wait to feel you again."

His attempt at exciting her with his gestures and comments were like poison to her. The very sight of Peter made her skin crawl, and she began to wonder if the Governor was truly worth being forced into pleasuring this man whom she had rapidly grown to despise. Don Tatum was worth it to her. He was her fantasy, her goal in life, and this was the only direct way to a personal relationship with him.

After lunch, Shana and her boss checked into a classless motel room on the other side of town. The sleaziness of it only added to his excitement, and she saw that it turned him on to treat her like his own personal prostitute.

"Oh, baby, you are so sexy," he began talking dirty to her as if it was what she wanted to hear. "You make me so hot." His caresses on her skin only added to her illness, and she just wanted their rendezvous to be over with as quickly as possible.

After nearly an hour of his lascivious comments and revolting intimacy, she was grateful to finally have finished her duty to him. With the filth and disgrace that Shana felt, the smell of him on her was repulsive.

"I'm going to grab a quick shower before we go back to the office," she commented.

"No, I want you to feel me on you all day," he responded. "I'm just kidding, babe." Shana snarled with disgust as she attempted to rid herself of him.

After work that evening, Shana hurried home to a weekend of freedom from Peter Fallon. His twisted fantasies couldn't include her anymore. She needed to escape his control. Her days of being polite were gone, and in the week that would follow, she would have to be ruthless.

Soon, she was drowning her frustration in a bottle of Scotch from her liquor cabinet.

"You son of a bitch!" She yelled out to an imaginary Peter Fallon. "I'm not your whore, you womanizing bastard!" In a drunken slur of her words, she vowed revenge on him.

Her thoughts then turned to the Governor. "I love you, Don," she professed in her empty living room, as if he was standing before her. "We'll be together soon, darling. I promise," Shana slurred. "I'm going to make you the happiest man on Earth."

She couldn't wait a year for his assistant to retire, just to get to him. A year was far too long, and Shana wanted to insert herself into Don's life as quickly as possible. Her days were barren without the man that she loved by her side. Betty had to be ousted immediately, and she pondered a way to ensure that it happened. "It hurts me to have to do this, Betty, because I like you," Shana spoke in her alcohol-fueled haze. "You just happen to be in the wrong place at the wrong time." Ridding herself of Peter, alone, wouldn't get her close to Don. Betty was the one who needed to be ejected and since it appeared that she wouldn't be taking an early retirement, Shana would have to find another way.

When Sunday night arrived, she drove to the office. "Ms. Bradley, what are you doing here?" The night guard asked.

"Hi Carl," she responded with a friendly smile. "I was snuggled up on my couch when I suddenly remembered a presentation that I have in the morning, so I had to drag myself over here to get some work."

"I see," he replied. Would you like me to walk you to your desk?"

"Oh, thanks, but no, I'll just be a minute," she told him politely. Shana scurried, discreetly, to Betty's desk and, after a glance around the office to ensure that she was alone, she retrieved a wrench from her purse and quickly loosened the bolts on Don's assistant's chair. "Sorry, Betty," she ruefully spoke, "but at least you'll be compensated well." On her way out, she grabbed an empty folder from her desk.

"Thanks, Carl," she told the guard, flashing him the folder. "Have a good night."

"Good night, Ms. Bradley," he replied, peering up briefly from his book with a wave. With a grin on her face, Shana couldn't wait for the morning. Soon, she would be Don's personal assistant.

In bed that night, she dreamed of the future with the man that she adored. Working with him each day and going home to him every night was her goal in life. She needed to be with him, as his lover, his wife, forever.

Chapter 4

"Today's the day," she told her reflection in the mirror early the next morning. At the office, an ambulance awaited Betty, and Shana was delighted to see that her plan had worked. Inside, a small crowd was gathered near her, and two paramedics prepared a gurney as she screamed out in pain. The Governor stood over her, offering sentiments of consolation to his assistant. It was Shana's opportunity. She rushed over to Betty in a dramatic act of concern that could have easily won an award.

"Oh no, Betty!" She exclaimed. "Are you alright? What happened?"

"Her chair gave out on her," Don replied with worry in his voice. Finally, he had acknowledged her, she thought.

"Is she okay?" Shana asked the paramedics but received no response as they carried her to the ambulance with Don in quick pursuit.

The remainder of the work day was engulfed with chatter and speculation about Betty's accident, and Shana grew increasingly tense with the fear of being accused. She did her best to continue her work, elusively, and giggled in silence at the sight of a few other staff members examining their own chairs for fear of an incident like Betty's. To the best of her knowledge, no one in the office suspected her involvement in the accident. Her plan had evolved flawlessly, and she was well on her way to a new job title.

That evening, when she heard that the Governor was going to the hospital to visit his assistant, Shana made her way there also. Outside of Betty's room, she was halted by two suited security guards.

"You can go in momentarily," one told her with a firm and monotone voice, and she knew that it was because the Governor was in the room. She was taken aback, not expecting security to be escorting Don. Yet another opportunity to connect with him would pass her by.

Shana sat in the hospital cafeteria with a steaming cup of lightened coffee, carefully strategizing her plan to take Betty's position in the Governor's office. Don Tatum had no idea who she was, so how could she become his new assistant? Her method of achieving it had to be done tactfully. She couldn't rush in, overzealously, as if Betty had never mattered.

As she contemplated her strategy, the stroke of luck that she needed struck her. The Governor walked in, and he was alone. With great jubilation, she observed him greet the handful of people who remained in the cafeteria before finding a small corner table for himself and his coffee.

"This is my chance," Shana thought. Though she suspected that he didn't want to be interrupted, she couldn't let another opportunity elude her. She had to make her move. Slowly, with her heart racing and hands trembling, she approached him.

"Excuse me, Governor Tatum?" She timidly interrupted.

He glanced up from his newspaper with a polite smile and recognition of her. "Yes, hello."

"I'm terribly sorry to interrupt," she said. "My name is Shana Bradley, and I'm Peter Fallon's new assistant."

"Oh yes, I remember you from earlier today. You were there, with Betty." He stood with an extended hand. "Please, sit down."

"Are you sure? You look a little busy." She was thrilled with his invitation.

"Not at all, please," he motioned to the empty chair at his table. To Shana's delight, he had taken the bait. "Were you here visiting Betty?"

"Actually, yes," Shana found her bashful, modest persona. "She's pretty much my only friend in the office since I'm still the new girl around there."

"Betty's a terrific lady and, frankly, my right hand," Don replied. "I hate that this happened to her."

"Me too," Shana agreed. "I hope that she'll make it back to the office soon." After an awkward moment of silence, she made a sudden change of the subject. "How is your campaign coming along? I worked at the headquarters before I started in your office."

"Ah, I thought you looked familiar. I remember now," Don responded with a nod. "The campaign is going well and everyone is working very hard, as always."

"I'm very glad to hear that because I, sir, am your biggest supporter, by far," she flashed an enticing grin. "What you do for this great state of ours and its people are truly phenomenal."

"Well, thank you, and I hope to be able to continue it for another term." He glanced at the silver watch on his wrist. "Oh, I apologize, but I have to run. I'm late for dinner and my wife will have my head," he snickered, rising to his feet. "Ms. Bradley, it was very nice talking to you, and I'm sure that I will be seeing you around the office."

"You, too, Governor, and please, call me Shana," she replied as he made his exit. With contentment, she merrily made her way home. She was thrilled to have finally achieved a one on one conversation with Don Tatum. The ground work had been set for her plan to be carried out, and she was overjoyed.

"It won't be long, now, sweetheart," she thought to herself. "We'll be together, soon, and nothing will ever come between us."

"Terrible thing that happened to Betty, huh?" Peter commented to Shana at the office the following day.

"Yes, it's awful," she replied innocently as he flashed a suspicious stare. "I hope she'll be back soon."

"Do you really, Shana?" She glanced up from her desk with mystification on her face. "I know that you were in here, late, the night before her accident." Her heart was explosive with panic as she wondered how much he really knew. He couldn't have seen her loosen the bolts. Shana had made certain that no one was around. How did Peter know that she was even there that night?

"What exactly are you trying to imply, Peter?" Irritation invaded her paranoia.

"Come on, Shana, I think you and I both know what happened to Betty was no accident and hey, I have to commend you on your technique. Very innovative. I'm actually impressed." His suspicions, though accurate, couldn't be proven, and she refused to confess.

"I don't know what you're talking about, Peter, but I really don't like your accusations, especially given your lack of information," she told him. "Now, if you'll please excuse me, I have work to do." She peered into his fascinated eyes, a warning for him to keep his silence.

"When are we getting together again?" He whispered. His suspicion of her only seemed to intensify his sexual interest.

"That's over," she insisted firmly.

"Not if you intend to keep your job." His intentional slyness brought a showy smile to his face in recognition that he maintained authority over her. "Besides, we don't want everyone to know that poor old Betty is in the hospital because of you, do we?" Shana fumed at his threat and approached him, her face in his.

"Let me tell you something," she warned. "Bad things can happen to anyone." She stepped back and glared at him with somber lasers.

"I love a woman who knows what she wants," he told her. "See, I get what I want, also, so the deal is you either comply or what really happened to Betty might happen to slip out to the Governor, the police, and everyone else in town, got it?" He raised his brows for her answer. Shana had to admit that she had met her match in Peter Fallon. He had her completely figured out, and there was little that she could do about it. If she didn't meet his demands, he could ruin her, and whether she liked it or not, he did hold the power over her. With a sigh of defeat, she agreed with a nod.

Two days later, Don returned to his office and Shana made a point to see him. "I'm so sorry to bother you, Governor," she said after knocking on his door.

"It's no bother at all, Ms. Bradley. What can I help you with?"

"Actually, I just came to offer my assistance to you," she answered with a self-assured smile. "I realize that with Betty out, you must be bogged down, so if I can be of any help, please don't hesitate to ask."

He removed his glasses in consideration while peering up at her. "If you mean that, I could use some help with a couple of things, but I don't want to take away from any of your other work." Shana insisted on aiding Don in any way that she could, and back to her desk, she carried a small stack of papers to work on for him. At the end of the day, Peter stopped at her desk on his way out of the office.

"I'll see you tonight at your place," he commanded with a wink, and a reluctant nod of agreement from her confirmed it. Shana detested every detail of Peter Fallon, not only his flirtatious winks, but the perversion in his eyes, the sly smirk he carried, the overgrown ego that made him feel superior. She hated everything about him. Worst of all, he had her trapped in a game that she couldn't manage to escape. She was forced to be at his beckoning call and meet his every demand or he would see to it that her own game met an abrupt and detrimental end.

The thrill seemed to intensify more for Peter with each rendezvous that he and Shana had, almost as if she fed his influence. For days after each encounter, he appeared to glide on air and the sight nauseated her. Having to pleasure him nearly every week, for her, was nothing more than a chore, an emotionless task that was part of her job description. Even as much as she despised it, their encounters were becoming routine and almost normal to her.

"Shana, the work that you've done for me is impeccable," the Governor complimented. "I really appreciate your help."

"It's my pleasure," she gleefully replied with a proud smile.

"Betty has to have a hip replacement and will be taking an early retirement, so I'll need someone to take her place, if you're interested." Shana's eyes widened as butterflies danced within her. The Governor's offer serenaded her ears and nourished her elated soul.

"I would be truly honored to work with you, Governor Tatum." She couldn't erase the grin from her face, tempted to scream out with joyous song.

"Wonderful! I'll talk to Peter and have you start Monday morning," he informed her. Suddenly, Shana found freedom, no longer in Peter Fallon's clutches. His reign over her would cease, leading her from his twisted game of manipulation. The world had just been lifted from Shana's shoulders as she imagined the possibilities of her new position with the Governor. It was an enormous leap into his personal life, and her fantasies ran wildly through her mind. Working with Don, she felt, was sure to bring them increasingly closer, making anything possible. This was her golden opportunity to make the impression of a lifetime, one that would change both of their lives forever.

It was the weekend, and Shana clad herself in her favorite black cocktail dress to celebrate her promotion at a local bar with her friend, Carla. As always, every male eye examined her when she came through the door as the women peered resentfully. They had barely sat down before drink offers from several men around them poured in, each competing for her attention. She savored the adoration from those around her while Carla grinned, enviously, at their prey.

"How do you do it?" Carla inquired with a giggle.

"Shana Bradley," a familiar male voice spoke behind her. She turned to see Mark, an attractive, athletic man in his thirties whom she had dated the previous year.

"Mark, hi," she greeted with an innocent smile.

"How is the woman who broke my heart?" His smile shone light and truth in every woman's soul in town. Mark was gorgeous with his sand-colored hair and baby face, and Shana had always found him difficult to resist. He was once the love of her life and always the one that got away.

"Oh, stop it," she blushed. "I'm doing great and, in fact, I'm here celebrating my new position as Governor Tatum's assistant." Her impressed former flame lifted his beer.

"A toast, to a beautiful woman and a bright future."

"Cheers to that," she responded, lifting her glass. Her heart fluttered with feelings of her past with him.

"I've always felt that you were the one who got away, Shana, and I kick myself for letting you go so easily," Mark told her. "What do you say we go somewhere and talk for a while?"

It was obvious to her that he wanted to do more than just talk and, though she did ponder an encore with him, she resisted his invitation.

"Oh what, are you dating the Governor or something?" He asked, and her sober stare gave him his answer. "You're dating the Governor?" Both he and Carla glared at her with astonishment.

Shana leaned in to him. "He's the best sex I've ever had," she replied and grinned at Mark's offended face. "Next time, don't let a woman who loves you get away so easily."

"Wow, I envy you so much," Carla told her friend with an amused giggle.

"Men are just easy targets," she replied, sending them both into a roar of laughter.

Chapter 5

Early on Monday morning, Shana proudly took her place at Betty's desk, outside of the Governor's office, rearranging the drawers to make the space her own. Carefully, she placed all of Betty's photo frames and belongings into a small box to be delivered to her that evening.

"Well, I see that you're all moved in," a lanky, brown-haired lady in her forties commented with a hint of sarcasm. "I'm Johanna Fields, assistant to Mrs. Tatum." Shana rose with a kind handshake, surprised that Felicia required an assistant of her own.

"Nice to meet you. I assume that we'll be working pretty closely together from now on."

"Yes, well, Betty and I became quite close," she replied in her uppity tone as her eyes evaluated her competition. "There's a formal gathering at the Governor's residence in two weeks, so we'll need to get together and do some planning. Since we're in a time crunch, we need to get on it as soon as possible." Johanna came off to Shana as domineering and snooty. Her tone exuded superiority.

Shana's face lit up when the Governor arrived and greeted her. "You're looking quite handsome today," she bravely complimented. She loved the way his hair held a slight dampness from his morning shower. With a glance of surprise, as if her comment was out of line, he explained that they had a hectic day ahead.

"You may even have put in a couple of late evenings," he informed her.

"Oh, I don't mind at all," she replied willingly. Shana looked forward to the nights alone with Don and the possibilities that they could bring. It could only pave her path to a personal relationship with him. She gloriously breathed in the sweet scent of his cologne each time he walked by her and it made her craving for him even stronger.

After spending most of her next few days with Johanna, planning the gathering, Shana was exhausted and anxious to get home and relax, but her exit was interrupted by the familiar hounding of Peter Fallon.

"Just because you're Don's assistant now doesn't mean you can just avoid me," he joked.

"Well, I just haven't had time to . . ."

"Make time," he abruptly intervened. "Don't forget our deal, Shana." Peter still possessed the influence to ruin her life, and his need to wield it was overpowering.

"Alright, listen, Peter," she said. "This has to stop. I can't keep this up anymore." With a cunning snicker, he flashed a patronizing glare.

"Well then, I'll just take the time to remind you that you are only here because of me and that can change at my discretion." His pompous character sickened her and she was fed up with his ego.

"And I'll take the time to remind your wife why you're not home when you should be," Shana barked. "Then, I'll remind my new boss, the Governor, about the sexual harassment laws in this country and how they are being broken right inside of his office."

"Don't forget about what happened to Betty," he threatened.

"Don't you forget that worse things can happen to anyone at any time," she subtly rebuffed with raised eyebrows before walking away, proudly. It was an enormous relief to finally be free of Peter's manipulative ploys, and she felt wonderful.

The week that followed consisted of hours of preparation with Johanna for the soiree at the Governor's residence, where he and other government officials would gather for a blend of business and pleasure. With her knowledge and expertise in previous events, Johanna assumed control with Shana as her obedient partner. Taking a secondary role was difficult for her since she had always assumed control in everything that she did, and Felicia's assistant wasn't making it any easier, barking commands like a four-star general. Shana loathed her pretentiousness, Johanna's way of disparaging her. She relished her leadership far too much for Shana's liking.

"For all of our labor on this event, Governor and Mrs. Tatum always extend an invitation to us," Johanna explained, and Shana felt the immediate grasp of excitement overtake her. "It's a formal event, so you'll want to wear a nice gown . . . if you have one," she abashed. Shana was ecstatic to be invited to the Governor's social event. She looked forward to such a sensational event, where she could mingle with the town's finest – and richest - residents and, moreover, mingle with Don Tatum on a more personal level.

"Where do I get a fabulous gown around here?" She asked Carla on the phone. Shana needed an ensemble that would astonish and electrify those around her. It was imperative that she make a dignified impression.

Two hours and more than one hundred miles of driving led the two women to a larger world, where the people never rested and the shops were always bustling. Shana and Carla drifted through stores of the finest fashions in search of the perfect gown until at last, a magnificent sight mesmerized her. The long, tapered piece of royal blue silk was the attention-grabber that she needed for the Governor's party. She had found the dress that no woman could be overlooked in with its wrap of fine fur. The gown was stunning, as if created for a queen.

Hours before the event, Shana sat in a salon, having her hair and makeup impeccably prepared by her loyal friends, Carla and Sarah. "I have to look flawless," she told the duo.

"How exciting to be going to the Governor's mansion," Carla commented.

"Yes, well, Don and I have grown very close," Shana deceptively boasted with conceit, leaving the obvious implication of an affair between the two. The awe in the women's expressions exhilarated her as she thoughtlessly absorbed their envy.

With her transformation complete, Shana inspected her image in the wall-length mirror in the salon. Never before had she imagined herself so exquisite, like a magnificent porcelain doll. She was amazed at what she saw.

"You look like a princess," Carla complimented.

"I feel like a queen," she responded with appreciation.

Shana eagerly made her way to the Governor's mansion of magnificent white stone and impeccable floral gardens. A vibrantly lit fountain accented a circular, cobblestone driveway, where limousines delivered Indiana's most noble inhabitants. The notion of mingling with society's elite made her euphorically nervous but she was prepared to leave a lasting impression on each and every one of them.

Shana felt like the most refined royalty as she was gracefully led through the airy foyer into a glorious reception room of polished oak, fine marble floors and crystal vases of fragrant bouquets within ornamented walls of fine art. The room's splendor made her wonder what the personal quarters of the mansion held.

A mass of superbly dressed politicians, each with his mate by his side and a champagne glass in his grasp, quickly packed the room. Shana made her grand entrance, breezing slowly through the door to allow every eye to notice her. She stares of many men in the room followed her sashay through while subtle whispers ensued among a slew of the guests. Surely, she exuberated importance among them, she thought, and they all sought an answer to the mystery of who she was. Shana savored her position as the center of attention.

Only seconds had passed before she was approached by a trio of middle-aged wives, curiously probing her identity for their next season of gossip.

"I'm the Governor's new assistant," Shana proudly informed the women.

"Oh, well, young and beautiful," one commented pretentiously. "I'm sure Felicia is thrilled to have you on board."

"Tell me, Shana, exactly what do you do for Governor Tatum?" Another probed suspiciously.

When their introduction ended as quickly as it began, she watched them scurry to report their new information to the other inquisitive female guests. Their jealousy only reiterated to her how much of a threat she really was to them and seeing them scold their husbands for ogling brought on a grin.

"Well, Shana, you look . . ." Johanna took a step backward to evaluate her colleague, ". . . fabulous." There was little sincerity in her tone but Shana was gracious nonetheless.

"Thanks," she smiled, looking at Johanna's red strapless dress. "You do, as well." After a brief scan of the spacious, society-filled room, she continued. "Have you seen Governor Tatum yet?"

The woman led her through the droves to the opposite end of the room, where Don stood with his dazzling wife, smiling and socializing with his guests. Immediately, his assistant caught his fascination and the glare of Felicia.

"Shana, welcome. Glad you could make it," he greeted with his usual friendly face. "This is my lovely wife, Felicia." He turned to explain to her that Shana was his new assistant.

"So nice to meet you," Felicia said warmly with a handshake while peering cautiously at her new acquaintance.

"You, as well, Mrs. Tatum," she replied with her most sincere smile. "I've heard wonderful things about you, and I truly admire the work that you do." Though her words were fallacious, Shana needed to earn Felicia's trust if she was to get closer to Don without being guarded.

"Well now, don't you let my husband turn you into a workaholic like himself," she ribbed with a glance at him.

"Oh, I don't mind at all," Shana told her with an echoed sentiment. "I am committed to his needs." She was committed to all of his needs and his wife already appeared to suspect it.

A short time later in the evening, Shana noticed that she had been spotted by Peter Fallon, who toted his socialite wife on his arm. She could see the couple mingling their way toward her as she glided the opposite direction to avoid them. Eventually, the Fallons caught up to her.

"Shana, you remember my wife, Darlene," Peter said while, inconspicuously, studying her assets.

"Hello, darling," she greeted in an uppity tone with her hand out as if Shana should kiss it. She was vivid and tout. "I've heard that you and Peter have grown pretty close the last few months." Shana's eyes amplified with fear as she glared at her former boss.

"I taught her everything I know around the office," he smirked as Shana struggled to pull herself together.

"He's such a great man," Darlene told Shana as she admired her husband with her hand on his cheek.

"If you only knew the truth," Shana wanted to tell her. It was apparent that Darlene didn't know the seedy hound that Peter really was. His wife, so focused on her position in society, was completely oblivious to his actions.

The few weeks that followed slowly closed the gap between Shana and Governor Tatum. Working long hours together lent them time for small talk and getting to know each other better as he asked questions about her life and family, who lived out west. Don frequently chatted with her about his wife and children. Seven year old Joseph played soccer and was slated to become a prominent doctor while five year old Shannon doted on ballet. Felicia was a successful attorney and active socialite within the community.

"I don't see her as much as I'd like," Don said of her. "She works even longer hours than I do."

Shana was taken by surprise to discover how modest the governor was when he was relaxed and, soon, it was obvious to her that Don only carried a dignitary's persona when surrounded by his staff. Her presumption that he was intense and dry-humored, she discovered, was far from the truth when his boyish wit peeked out.

"I never knew you had it in you," Shana told him with astonishment.

"Is it a rule that the governor has to be uptight and emotionless?" He asked. "I'm still just an average guy."

"That's a great thing, and I think people would be pleased to know that about you when they re-elect you for another term," Shana replied. "People, sometimes, tend to view politicians as counterfeit and, this way, they could see that you're just like them, you know?"

"That's it!" He exclaimed when the idea struck him. "That's the edge that I need in my campaign, that I'm one of them, working for them."

He glared at his assistant with appreciation for her idea. "Shana, you are brilliant!"

"Well, why don't we go get some Chinese food and work on it a little?" She suggested with a proud grin.

"Chinese food?"

"Well, if you plan to use this new slogan, you have to be able to back it up, which you can't do at fine dining establishments."

"You're right. Let's go."

Over their cartons of fried rice, Lo Mein, and orange chicken that the pair had taken back to the Governor's office, they mapped out an agenda for his new campaign slogan.

"I think it's very noble of you to show your authenticity to the world like this," Shana complimented her boss on a more serious level. She stared intently into his bright blue eyes with admiration and she swore that he was blushing.

"I appreciate you bringing out that side of me because it's easy to lose your true identity in what others expect of you." His gracious smile grew sober as he boldly returned her stare, his eyes peering into hers as if searching for her soul. It was obvious to Shana that Don felt the intensity of their attraction, as her heart pounded like thunder, and she had to use it to her advantage before it slipped away. Gradually, she drew closer and with her soft caress, she timidly stroked his cheek.

"I crave you," she whispered and closed her eyes for the greatest gift of her life. His lips were velvet ecstasy on hers as she kissed the man of her dreams with a soft passion, her heart fluttering from her chest to her stomach as they melted into one another. He enveloped her, tightly, in his masculine embrace, as if never willing to let go, and it was the most comfortable feeling of her entire life.

"You're amazing," he complimented, tenderly, before reconvening their embrace. His sentiment lit her soul ablaze. Hungrily, Shana held on to her man, squeezing him firmly against her, as if fusing into him, as her libido screamed out wildly for his attention.

"I need you," she moaned, unbuttoning his blue dress shirt to reveal his bronzed and chiseled midsection, an alluring attraction for her mouth. Her hands gently traced every inch of him as he slowly removed her blouse, his lips savoring her neck. His pants fell to the floor, revealing utter perfection. Don's cries of ecstasy lit Shana afire as he savored her with his mouth, and the danger of being caught, half-naked, on the brown leather sofa in the Governor's patriotic-themed office intensified the thrill. For the moment, all either of them needed was each other and never had someone excited her so much in all of her life. She wanted to make euphoric love with him forever, seemingly unable to fulfill herself of him, but she could erupt at any moment while she squealed in erotic bliss until soon, he, too, echoed her rumblings in a full explosion.

The ill-fated couple lay, awestruck and catching their breath in recovery after the most electrifying encounter either had ever experienced.

"I can't believe we just did that," Don erupted in amusement, never having dared such a thing, as his assistant giggled. Heaven had finally found her.

"You were so incredible," Shana told her lover as he held her in his arms, gently stroking her back. She wished that they could stay like that for eternity.

He lifted his eyes to hers in a gaze that she swore beamed of love. "Shana, you revived me," he romantically confessed. "I'm suddenly so alive, which I haven't felt in years." His words rang true on both sides. They were a symphonic masterpiece playing in her ears.

"Now you're mine," she told him in silence as she savored the most incredible night of her life.

As they lay, talking, Don spoke of his once confident marriage which, throughout the years, had become unfulfilling and was held together only by their children.

"Our marriage is all a front," he confessed. "As the governor, I have to appear a wholesome and moral family man. That's what the world expects of me." With a sigh, he continued. "I don't think that she's happy, either, but she and our children are accustomed to the lifestyle and the symbol that we must represent." He stared at Shana with melancholy eyes and she yearned for the chance to reinvigorate him.

"I'm so sorry to hear that," she fibbed while hoping that his failing marriage increased their chances of a relationship.

"No, don't be sorry," he said. "You breathed life back into me. I feel alive with you, and your vitality shows me that anything is possible.

Somewhere in time, that escaped me, and I think I was just going through the motions. My only fervor was fed by my work as the governor but, now, you've reminded me that life holds so much more along with that."

"You've been my passion for so long," Shana confessed after analyzing Don's every word.

"And now, you're mine," he responded, lovingly, and delicately, his lips, again, found hers.

His kiss nourished her soul as she yearned for his attentive touch. In that moment, Don was hers, completely, and the rest of the world was nonexistent.

"I'll treat you like the amazing man that you are," Shana whispered in his ear while her lips traced his neck ever so softly.

Again, they made love, leisurely and passionately savoring one another. He was pure voltage to her body as the waves electrified her veins, stimulating her with his every spine-tingling movement. Shana knew that she needed him in her life. She loved him.

Chapter 6

In the days that followed, Shana walked with a jubilant spring in her step and wore a radiant grin on her face. Don had brought new meaning to her life. He walked on water and she soared atop the clouds with the euphoria of their blossoming romance. He was all she had ever deemed important in her life and having him meant everything to her.

None of their colleagues seemed to notice the pair's flirtatious glances and sexual insinuations and, for Shana, it was only the beginning of the extraordinary relationship that she had always dreamed of. Together, she felt, she and Don were unsurpassable pillars of envy who could easily prevail in the political realm. She imagined herself in Felicia's place, living splendidly in the governor's mansion, entertaining the upper class in lavish gowns and jewelry and enveloped, each night, in the secure arms of the well-respected man that she adored. Shana believed, wholeheartedly, that she was the next Mrs. Tatum. Don had told her that she had restored life in him, something his wife could never have done, and she was certain that it was only a matter of time before she stepped into her shoes.

Concentrating on her work became an increasingly daunting task when her lover was near. He was all that she could see, all that was in her mind. Shana wanted to yell out to the world that she was in love but she couldn't tell a soul.

Behind the closed door of the governor's oak ornamented office, the duo discreetly exchanged kisses and caresses, energized by the risk of being caught. Frequently, his mistress tantalized him with nothing but her thigh high hose beneath her skirt, thrilling the middle-aged politician with her naughty antics.

"I can't stop thinking about you lately," Don professed to her. "You drive me wild."

"Oh, really?" She responded, seductively straddling his lap and wanting him then and there. "Good because I like it that way." She breathed in the aroma of his cologne that she loved so much.

"I have to go out of town for a couple of days, and I want you to go with me."

"I'd love nothing more." Shana was ecstatic at the idea of spending two days alone with Don, where she could pretend to be his wife, catering to his every whim and sharing his bed at night. She planned to use the time to make him never want to let her go. There was no other woman, Shana felt, that could give the Governor what she could, and she was ready to prove it to him.

"But in the meantime . . ." He said, pulling her into the private restroom in his office. He locked the door and lifted her up on the sink with her skirt at her waist. "I need you right now."

"Enjoying your new job, I see," a familiar and chilling voice said, later in the day, and she knew, immediately, who it was. Reluctantly, she turned around to see Peter Fallon's eyes pleasurably scanning her body, nauseating her with ease. Shana wanted nothing to do with the scoundrel. "You're looking delicious, as always," he whispered with a sly wink and she desperately wanted to brag that his boss had just enjoyed her.

She peered at the stubby and balding man, wondering how he became so pompous. What was it in him that empowered him with so much confidence? He glided around her with an act of suave decadence that he couldn't pull off nearly as well as he thought that he did.

"Well, you just can't seem to stay away, can you?" She replied sarcastically with a forced partial smile.

"I've been thinking about you a lot, and I need to see you again."

"I'm sorry, but that can't happen anymore," she replied with relief. "I'm dating someone now." He peered at her in a short silence, as if in disbelief that she would betray him.

"I'm married but I don't let that interfere," he told her with the implication that she needed to make time for him. When Shana refused to see him again, Peter leaned in to her and whispered, "Considering what I know, I think that it's in your best interest that we get together very soon." He flashed her a look that insisted on her compliance.

Shana was cornered, once again, by his manipulation. It was true that Peter knew too much. He had ample information that could easily destroy her if he chose to publicize it. He knew that she had caused Betty's injury and she suspected that he was even aware of her budding relationship with the Governor. Peter had the ability to ruin her entire life if she didn't comply with his demands, and she despised him for it. The only way to keep him from coming between Don and her was to comply.

"Alright, you win. We'll get together again," she agreed, "but I'm leaving tomorrow for a business trip so it will have to be when I get back." He glared at her with a satisfying grin of pride that he had, once again, gotten what he wanted from her. Shana wondered how he could still be so happy with the idea of being with her, even knowing that she loathed him. "I won't enjoy it."

"You don't have to because I'll enjoy it enough for both of us," he smugly smirked. "I'll see you later. Oh, and Shana, have fun with your new boyfriend, but don't forget who you really belong to." Peter seemed to indulge in the torment that he caused.

As she watched him walk away, proud of his actions, anger seared her face, and she felt like lasers would shoot out of her eyes. She needed to rid herself of Peter's perversion-filled fantasies but, as long as he was armed with the information that he had against her, she would be forced into submission. With his knowledge of her affection for the Governor, she knew that their relationship would surely be his first target, and she wasn't about to let anyone interfere with her dream of being Don Tatum's wife. Something had to be done to stop Peter Fallon's tactics.

That evening, as she packed for her excursion with the Governor, Shana searched her mind for a plan to rid herself of Peter for good. It needed to be something permanent that he could never speak of. There was only one thing that could be done, she told herself.

She quickly switched her thoughts back to Don. Her trip with him was her opportunity to truly prove her love and devotion. She needed to make him feel what she felt, and she had to make him commit to her. Now he was hers, and she couldn't bear the thought of ever losing him. He was the love of her life and it seemed that everything she did was for him. He was her motivation, her reason for living. This would be her chance to clench their relationship with a lifelong obligation. Shana was certain that she could make it happen. Don had made his feelings for her obvious already so sealing the deal seemed an easy task. She lay in bed with images of her fantasy dancing gleefully through her mind. Visions of the two of them alone together, dancing and kissing, Don professing his unwavering adoration for her. Shana was certain that, by the time the trip ended, the Governor would be ready to

61

divorce his wife for her. She was well on her way to being the new Mrs. Tatum.

On the private plane to Washington, D.C. with some of the Governor's staff members which, to Shana's dismay, included Peter Fallon, she and Don were forced to keep their flirtations hidden and their interaction solely professional for the sake of business. Don sat with his Chief of Staff, discussing their plan for their upcoming meeting at the White House as Shana, inconspicuously, eyed him with admiration, longing for his attention. He was a different man with her, uninhibited and adventurous. When they were alone together, Don wasn't the Governor but a spontaneous child at play. On the plane, he was nothing short of professional, expertly discussing business with his colleagues, each attentive to his words. Shana admired the distinguished authority in him and she adored his modesty.

From the corner of her eye, she caught the perversion-filled stares of Peter, hungrily ogling her from his nearby seat on the plane, and he didn't seem to care who was watching. He looked as if he would ravage her at any moment, and his piercing eye discomforted her. She hoped that he wouldn't hound her during their stay, though she wondered if she was the reason that he decided on taking the trip after all. Shana regretted even telling him that she was going. All that she could do was try her best to avoid him during the trip, but she knew it would be a challenge given the fantasies already in his head.

"When we land in the Capital, I would like to get a couple hours of rest, alone, so any business that we have, let's take care of now or later this evening," the governor politely commanded his staff, and Shana hoped that his comment was meant to give him some private time with her. When he turned to flash a flirtatious raise of his brows, she returned him a pleased grin.

They checked into their hotel suites and a half hour later, when he felt that everyone had settled in, the governor beckoned his mistress to his room, the personal invitation that she had been anxiously awaiting. Shana blissfully made her way to Don with lacy, blue lingerie under her clothes and adventure on her mind. He made her want to be spontaneous and exciting and she knew that he relished it. She wanted to give him everything that his wife wouldn't and keep him coming back for more.

"Let me ask you something, Governor," she said, seductively, pulling him closer to her by his striped tie. "Do you like naughty girls?" His mistress revealed her surprise.

"Wow!" He exclaimed with bulging eyes that scanned her. He was mesmerized by Shana's tanned physical perfection and sex appeal, and he thrived on her need to excite him.

After more than an hour of explosive passion, Shana lay, blissfully, in the arms of the man she adored, wishing that they could stay that way forever. "I love you," she fearlessly confessed to him and, though he chose a kiss over echoing her words, she felt that he loved her also.

"You amaze me, Shana," Don said with a soft tone. "You're different – exciting and so free.

You stimulate me and make me feel . . .", he searched for the ideal word, ". . . appreciated."

"I feel the same," Shana told him. "You deserve to feel like the man you really are, and you need someone to give you that appreciation and spontaneity."

"I need you," the Governor professed. "I need you in my life." Don's words always exhilarated her like a drug comforted an addict. She hung on to his every comment, analyzing each one a million different ways, and she was sure that he was falling for her.

Later that evening, Governor Tatum and his staff sat in an exclusive restaurant, discussing their upcoming visit to the White House the following day. Shana admired his intellect and refinement as he spoke. She understood, clearly, why he was so well respected among everyone who knew him, or even knew of him.

"Speaking of my campaign, Shana, I'd like for you to oversee the committee at headquarters. She worked with the campaign team before starting with us in the office," he told his colleagues.

"Absolutely," she answered with what she hoped was a respectable overtone of professionalism. Don kept his public conversations with her strictly business and, as far as either he or Shana could tell, none of the others suspected a relationship between them. Peter, however, wasn't one of them. He always seemed to find out all of her inhibitions sooner or later and his knowledge made her nervous. With him on the trip, Shana had to be extremely judicious about her time with the governor.

As always, she felt Peter's eyes evaluating her with his inappropriate thoughts, and it infuriated her. Don could never know about her and Peter, but his continuous winks and grins were painfully obvious, she feared. With his eyes glued to Shana, he arose and casually made his way to her side of the table.

"I need to see you tonight, baby," he whispered in her ear as she pretended that it was merely business. "You are looking so tasty." His words made her ill and she would make up any excuse not to see him, especially since her attention was on his boss.

"Um, I'm not sure," she replied aloud with a professional mannerism. "I'll have to get back with you on that."

He peered around to the eyes of his coworkers on the two of them. "Fantastic, but I'll need the information soon, okay?" He responded to his lover in a professional tone.

"Of course," she replied with a forced smile, grateful to be let off the hook.

Back in the governor's suite, she and Don playfully bathed together in the shell-shaped Jacuzzi with soft ballads and the flicker of candlelight in the background, when her cell phone began to ring.

"Do you need to get that?" Don queried, but Shana knew it was Peter calling to request some time with her.

"No, you're all I'm trying to get right now," she giggled, rubbing her hands across his chest.

Again, the ringing of her phone attempted to spoil their quest as they sat, entwined in a passionate kiss.

"Are you sure you don't want to get that? It might be important," Don said.

"It's not important," his mistress insisted, continuing her quest. When her phone rang three more times within the five minutes that followed, a frustrated Shana stomped over to turn it off. Peter's constant calls incensed her more with each one, but she was determined to proceed with her rendezvous with Don, without interruption.

The next morning, after breakfast, the governor and his staff prepared for their meeting at The White House. He pulled his assistant aside to hand her his personal credit card.

"Go do some shopping," he told her, softly, and she peered at him with bewilderment. To her consternation, Shana wasn't invited to their meeting, as she had expected to be. "I'll see you in a couple of hours. Get something really sexy for tonight, too, okay?"

Though she was disappointed to not be going to the White House with Don and the other men, Shana was thrilled about the alternative. "Take me shopping," she told the limo driver.

Several hours of buying bliss followed, in all of the top-rated stores, and afterward, Shana lay on the couch in the Governor's suite, in a sheer white negligee, awaiting his return. She couldn't wait for her lover to arrive. He walked in with a glimmer in his eyes and a grin carved on his face to see the young beauty sprawled out before him, and they spent their final night making passionate love in the nation's capital.

The thought of Don returning home to his wife tormented Shana. She loved him and wanted him all to herself. His wife, she felt, couldn't possibly love him like she did, and she couldn't make him truly happy the way that Shana did. She struggled to understand what kept their marriage together. What did he really see in her? The mere thought of Don kissing and holding his wife burned her with betrayal. She felt that he belonged to her and for him to be with another woman, even his wife, was as if he was cheating on her. In Shana's world, it was Mrs. Tatum who was the mistress.

"What happened to you last night?" Peter probed Shana with a whisper on the plane, back to Indiana. "I called you numerous times and got no answer."

"Well, I went to bed early," she fibbed, still unable to dismiss his constant advances. "I think the wine at dinner got to me a little."

"Tonight then," he commanded with the anticipation of seeing her and, though she agreed, Shana had no intention of making good on it. The time had come to put her plan into action. When Peter didn't show up that night, she knew that it had worked.

"He's in the hospital," Peter's new assistant informed Shana when she went in search of him the following day. "Car accident."

She put on an alarmed face, hoping to appear sincere. "That's awful," she replied with a tone of concern. "How is he?" His assistant explained that Peter was in a coma with swelling of the brain and several broken bones.

"The doctors don't know if he'll pull through. He's in critical condition right now."

Though Shana felt a twinge of guilt over loosening the brakes on her former boss's car, freeing herself of his incessant torture was as if a weight had been lifted from her shoulders. No longer would she have to endure Peter's relentless manipulation and persecution, and she was as a bird escaping from its cage. It was exhilarating. With Peter out of the way, Shana could focus on Don, completely, while keeping all of her secrets safe.

The news of Peter's accident was announced on every newspaper and television station in Indiana as its residents absorbed the jolt of the terrible tragedy and prayed for his recovery.

"Police are investigating but say, at this time, that the accident appears to be a result of faulty brakes on his car," the news reporter on television stated. "It isn't immediately clear where Peter Fallon was headed when the crash occurred." An uneasy Shana breathed relief with the reporter's words. She had to ensure that no one knew of her involvement with Peter. Not a soul could find out that he was headed to her house before his accident and that it was she who was responsible for the crash. It had to appear accidental.

"We're on a downward spiral with employees around here," the Governor remarked to his assistant. "First Betty and now Peter."

"I know, it's awful," she replied with counterfeit grief.

"I'm going to the hospital this afternoon to offer my condolences so maybe I'll stop by your place afterward?" Shana nodded her head with an excitable grin, anxious for some time with Don.

"Definitely. I'll be waiting."

In her apartment, she watched as the news stations reported the latest updates on Peter's unchanged condition. He remained in a coma with injuries so severe that they threatened his life. Suddenly, she was repentant for her actions, but Shana felt that she had been left with no other alternative. Peter knew too much. He had found out that she was the cause of Betty's injury, and she suspected that he also knew of her affair with the governor. As long as he possessed the information, she could never free herself of him. His accident was her only escape and, in her mind, it had to be done. He lay, on the verge of death, and it tested her conscience. Her intention wasn't for him to die, but she wondered what would happen if he recovered. Would he be the same person that he was before the accident? Would he tell what he knew about her or would he even remember any of it?

The police investigation into the accident rattled her nerves. Even though she had taken extreme precaution, she worried that they would discover Peter's car being tampered with. Still, she thought, she had merely loosened his brakes and no one would ever be able to prove it.

Don soon arrived with despair in his eyes. "I almost didn't recognize him lying in that hospital bed," he told her despondently. "His wife looked so heartbroken and desperate, and I hardly knew what to even say to her." The Governor's face told a story of anguish over his assistant.

"I was just getting the latest update on the news but it said that his condition hadn't changed," Shana replied with an attempted condolence. "It's just awful."

Don took her in his arms, holding her closely against him. "There are so many uncertainties in life." His voice was faint and heartrending as he appeared to ponder his own life. "You just can't take anything for granted." Shana broke gently from his secure embrace and peered into his saddened eyes.

"It breaks my heart to see you like this," she said. "What happened to Peter is terrible but it was an accident. Even as horrible as it is, we just can't dwell on the tragedies of life because, if we did, we would be blinded to the blessings." She caressed his cheek with concern in her face and led him to the couch, where she held him, stroking his head. "Our days are numbered, and I think that all we can do is try to fill our lives with as much satisfaction and love possible while we're here. I strongly believe that all things happen for a reason, just like you and me."

The Governor broke from his pondering stare, into the air, to look into the eyes of his mistress and Shana could see him evaluating his feelings for her. "Do you love me?" His soft voice sang to her sweetly. It was the moment Shana had been waiting for. The word "love" had finally entered their dialogue and she knew that he asked out of his own love for her. Perhaps he was ready to leave his wife for her, just as she had always planned. Her heart told her that it wouldn't be long and she had been ready for a very long time.

"Of course I love you," she answered his question. "You're the only man I want in my life, my soul mate, and I've dreamed of us spending our lives together." She waited to hear his profession of love for her, as well, but he stared at her in silence. Don sat up with a sigh and it became obvious to Shana that his mind was a whirlwind of thoughts, as if he was searching his soul for answers.

"I've been so confused lately," he confessed as she peered into his eyes. "You are such an amazing woman, Shana. You've brought life back to me. You thrill me with your spontaneity and gregarious personality. You truly shine." Her eyes lit, joyously, with his golden words.

"You bring that out in me," she replied. "You give my whole life a glorious flutter, and you make me want to hand you the world. You're my breath, Don." Once again, Shana awaited his echo of her words, only to find his increasingly frequent silence. Why wasn't he saying it? She wondered. It should have already floated from his lips, effortlessly, but it was an apparent struggle for him to say. "Do you love me?" She asked him in an attempt to assist.

He took a deep breath and the most sorrowful face that she'd ever seen on him emerged. He cleared his throat.

"No," he whispered softly.

Chapter 7

Shana felt as if she had just swallowed her heart. How could this man that she devoted her life to not love her? She wondered. He said, himself, that she had breathed life back into him so how could he not love her? Her entire world began collapsing. Don glared at her with poignant eyes.

"I care so much for you. I really do, and I've never met anyone like you. I look forward to seeing you every day, and I even get that flutter in my stomach," he told his lover. "My marriage had grown lifeless and predictable, and she and I were just coexisting, for the image of it all, mostly, but seeing Peter in the hospital, fighting for his life, seeing his wife and children there, it flipped on a switch inside of me and made me consider my own family. It could be me in that hospital bed, and they could be my wife and kids hurting. It made me consider my own family, my own life." It wasn't the response that she had hoped for. Peter's condition was supposed to make Don realize that he needed the excitement of her over the staleness of his marriage.

"What are you saying?" Shana responded with agony and grief, but she knew the answer. Her plan had backfired.

"I'm saying that, even as much as I like you, Shana, I owe it to my family to work on my marriage."

Fury cultivated itself within her as she listened to Don's words and, aside from the enormous heartbreak, she felt deceived. He had used her only to throw her away as if she had never mattered to him at all. Tears seared her eyes as she struggled to grasp his decision, and she found herself without words and pain in her chest. The governor's sudden epiphany stung her. He had just ruined her entire life, solely with his words, and his wife took precedence. Shana's feelings seemed unimportant to him, and the realization that she had invoked his feelings by causing Peter Fallon's accident wounded her.

"Shana, I'm sorry," He apologized. "I truly didn't want to hurt you."

There was so much that she wanted to say to Don, so many thoughts racing through her head, but the devastation that she felt had kidnapped her words. She needed to make her lover understand how much she truly needed him.

"I can't lose you," were the only words that she could muster. Her eyes were liquid blue anguish and she couldn't remember a time of ever suffering more.

"Given the circumstances, it's imperative that we maintain a purely professional working relationship, without romantic intrusion." The governor uttered his words as if he had rehearsed them a hundred times over, as he would one of his speeches and, to Shana, they were impersonal, vacant of concern and compassion. She was incensed by his blatant disregard for her feelings, and she felt it unfair that he was making their relationship decisions, alone, as if she had no say at all.

"How can I pretend I don't love you, Don? I need you in my life. Why would you start this with no intention of finishing it? Do you really think that you can play with my emotions like that?" She needed him to feel her agony.

"It wasn't my intention for any of this to happen, Shana and, once again, I'm truly sorry." His sincerity wasn't enough for her and his decision wasn't acceptable. "I have to go," he said, making his way to the door as she pleaded for him to stay. Closing the door behind him signified the abrupt end of their relationship.

Scorned and heartbroken, Shana sobbed, uncontrollably, wondering how the man she loved could turn his feelings off so quickly and leave her as if she had never mattered to him. She felt as though he had just destroyed her future, her life. Shana had planned her world with Don in it. He was all she lived for, and she failed to understand how he couldn't see that she loved him more than his wife possibly ever could.

"His big epiphany came from Peter?" She said to herself. "I risked everything to get Peter out of the way for Don, and this is what I get in return?" Shana was in disbelief that the very thing that she had done to progress their relationship was exactly what had destroyed it. It had driven him back into the arms of his wife. Maybe his feelings would pass, she thought. After all, he had confessed to a loveless marriage when he had spoken of his wife. Surely their relationship couldn't be repaired that easily. The lifelessness of their marriage would, soon, reiterate that Shana was the best woman for him, and she was sure that he would come back to her. "You'll be missing me before you even get home," she uttered, still drying her tears.

Shana decided that she would make herself irresistible to the governor in the upcoming days. She would remind him what had first attracted him to her and show him what his wife didn't have that she did.

"You can't stay away from me," she reassured herself about her lover. "You crave passion and sex appeal, not a lifeless piece of gristle like her." Shana deemed his wife a materialistic and self-absorbed socialite who only concerned herself with status and the unwavering envy of her peers. She didn't deserve a man as amazing as Don, in Shana's opinion, and she didn't deserve the fabulous life that he provided her. "He's only there for the kids," she told herself. He had even admitted it to her.

Claiming illness, Shana took the next day off from work. Not only did she want Don to assume that she was too heartbroken to go in, but she wanted to go shopping for the things that would entice him when she returned.

Floating through one shop after another in admiration of its inventory, Shana tried on the most elite fashions, shoes and even accessories that her money could buy. She needed the finest if she was going to win Don back. When the Governor saw her, he would realize what he had let go of and beg to get her back. She had learned his taste and bought ensembles that she knew would be impossible for him to resist. She even bought his favorite perfume for added insurance.

Shana glided into her office the following day, pristinely dressed in her new snug, black miniskirt that she was certain would drive Don wild, her perfectly curled tresses gently swept up, exactly the way that he preferred. With a mist of his favorite aroma, she entered his office to greet him.

"Today is going to be hectic for us," he informed her in a professional tone. He appeared unaffected by her attempt to regain his affection, and it made her try even harder. As the governor reviewed the day's events with her, Shana nonchalantly raised her skirt, desperately craving his attention, but he continued on with business as if he didn't notice her motive. She was growing increasingly agitated from Don's intentional neglect, and she wondered how he could just ignore her as if she was nothing to him. How could he suddenly resist his obvious attraction to her? What had, a short time earlier, been so heated had abruptly grown so cold. Shana missed him and she couldn't fathom how he could pretend that he didn't miss her, too. It pained her to sit before the man that she loved, only to be shunned by him as if their relationship had never existed. Couldn't he see the agony in her, she thought. Didn't he miss her at all?

"How are things with your wife?" She probed. With a suspicious glance, the governor was rendered nearly speechless, searching for a delicate answer.

"Things are fine but, as I said before, we really need to keep our conversations on a professional level," he responded with sober eyes that only permitted a brief look.

"I just don't understand how you can pretend that we never had something together." He lay the papers in his hand on the desk and removed his glasses.

"Listen, Shana, if the two of us working together is too difficult, then perhaps we should consider a different position for you here," he stated matter-of-factly, and she didn't take the implication well. Fury infiltrated her. Not only was he neglecting her but he threatened her career as well. It was as if Don sought to remove Shana from every aspect of his life and it was a sword being lunged into her flesh. She found it impossible to reason with him.

"Forgive me for the severity of my actions, Don, but I guess I just don't recover as well as you do," his guilt-inflicting assistant told him. "I can't turn my feelings off but I don't want to lose this job either, so I assure you that I will do my best to keep our dialogue all business." Keeping true to her word would be more difficult than it sounded but she had to preserve job to remain close to him.

The days that followed dealt misery for Shana. Don had quickly reverted to his lifeless face, vacant of his smile, and his dull eyes that used to light up so brightly when they were together. He was rigid and barren, as if the life was being rapidly drained from him. He treated her as if she didn't matter, at all, to him, and her feelings didn't appear to play any part in his decision to end their relationship. Shana hadn't even been asked her opinion about any of it and his treatment was unacceptable to her.

"I won't be blatantly brushed aside as if I never mattered," she told herself. She would fight for the man that she loved and win back his heart, no matter what it took to do it. The Governor would quickly see that Shana was the better woman for him. After all, she thought, if his wife couldn't satisfy him before, what was so different now? "It won't take long for Don to run back to me."

Later in the week, Don requested that Shana make dinner reservations for him and a group of friends for that evening, and she fumed with jealousy. She belonged at the restaurant with them, rather than making the reservation, and it was betrayal in her eyes. She felt that he was intentionally rubbing it in her face that she wasn't welcome at the dinner, as if she wasn't good enough to even invite.

When the governor left his office, Shana began searching his desk drawers for her golden ticket. Through the stacks of papers, files and business cards, she carefully looked until finally, she found the spare brass key.

"While the cat's away, the mouse will play," she told herself with a devious grin and a tight clasp on the key.

Just after dark, that evening, Shana parked her car and walked two blocks to the Governor's mansion. It exhilarated her to use the key and enter with a private freedom like it was her own residence. As always, the immaculate quarters were impeccably adorned with the finest oak and marble accents throughout. Its spacious magnificence awed Shana as she slowly made her way through, imagining that it was hers. She relaxed, momentarily, on a small sofa of modern, white plush, perfectly poised in the formal living room, relishing its soft elegance. Leisurely, Shana drifted through the family room of expensive leather furniture and a breathtaking stone fireplace, caressing the pristine splendor of each one until she was led to the oversized kitchen of stainless steel and flawless marble. The Governor's mansion was the home that everyone dreamed of, a spectacular collection of lavish rooms that could only be fit for the upper class.

Don's office was an oak-filled treasure, ornamented with the American and state flags where the Bible sat on a small stand in front of them. Shana opened each drawer of his enormous desk, carefully sifting through its contents.

Lastly, she followed the wooden-accented winding staircase to the more personal areas of the Governor's home, where she was taken aback by his young daughter's doll-filled, princess-themed room, as well as his teen son's sports-themed abode. Shana glided past two guest rooms, a book-filled den and two large, marble-accented bathrooms before entering the room that piqued her interest the most.

The master suite was a castle of delicate exquisiteness with its soft splendor of warmth and inviting aura of pleasure. Shana lay gently on the Governor's perfectly made bed, immediately finding the scent of him on one side. She dreamed of lying next to him at night, snugly cupped within his comforting embrace. She would give nearly anything to step into his wife's place. The copious walk-in closet displayed a plethora of colorful designer fabrics. Stunning gowns of silk and satin hid quaintly within high dollar garment bags while a masterpiece of posh shoes lined an entire wall. Shana couldn't fathom having the luxuries that she felt the family probably took for granted every day. She wouldn't have been surprised to find an authentic, jeweled tiara lying around. The intense envy sat on her lips as she cursed her foe for having the very life that she craved. She was desperate to sever the governor's marriage and replace his wife.

In the pockets of several of Don's suits, Shana placed a pair of lace panties, in hopes of his wife discovering them. She needed to wreak havoc in their already fragile relationship if her plan was to be successful.

Back in his home office, she planted false names and phone numbers of numerous women that she had made up. After all, Don's wife wouldn't call them. Discovering the numbers of other women would be enough to cause turmoil within their marriage. A desk drawer yielded one of his credit cards. Shana placed herself at his laptop computer, ordering herself bouquets of roses and flowers before a stop at the online jewelry store. Several diamond pieces later, her task was complete and she returned the card where it had come from.

"If Don wants to act like a womanizer, then he'll look like one too," Shana thought to herself as she deviously continued to plant evidence around the couple's sacred home. After returning to his closet to mist a few of his ties with her perfume, the Governor's mistress finished off her endeavor by rubbing her lipstick off on the collar of one of the Governor's shirts.

Chapter 8

Early on Monday morning, Shana discreetly stepped into the Governor's office to replace the spare key to his mansion before returning to her desk. She had already made two copies of the key made for future endeavors. Enthusiasm pierced her as she anxiously awaited Don's arrival. She was certain that his wife had discovered his infidelity by that time and couldn't wait to find out what had occurred between them over the weekend. There was no legitimate explanation that he could give for all of the evidence.

"Good morning, Shana," Johanna greeted in her usual condescending tone. "Has the governor arrived yet?" Since she was Mrs. Tatum's assistant, Shana could only assume that Felicia would now command Johanna to check up on her husband frequently.

"No, I haven't seen him since Friday afternoon, but I can certainly have him contact you when he gets in this morning," Shana replied with a forced smile of politeness.

"Um, no, that's okay," she replied, secretively. "I'll just check back with him later."

"Yes, I'll bet you will," Shana thought with a satisfied sneer on her face.

"By the way, do you know what his schedule looks like today?" The question was an obvious attempt for Johanna to probe her for information for his wife.

"I'm sorry, I won't know until he comes in." Shana refused to give the snooty assistant any satisfaction, especially when she wasn't even giving Shana enough credit to know what she was really up to. "Oh, but if I recall correctly, I do believe that the governor has a long lunch planned today," she fibbed, just to reaffirm Mrs. Tatum's suspicions. The accomplished look on Johanna's face as she walked away sent Shana into a giggle. "Now that she thinks she's actually gotten one over on me, she can get through the day," Shana snickered.

She had been busily working at her desk for two hours when Don dragged himself past her to his office. With his ruffled suit and weary eyes, he looked as if he hadn't slept all night, and Shana knew that her plan had worked.

"He and his beloved wife were probably up, arguing, all night," she thought to herself.

"Can you come in here for a minute, please?" The governor peered out of his office with a stern face.

"Good morning," his assistant greeted as she sat with him. "Are you feeling alright? Forgive me, but you appear a little under the weather today."

"Actually, I'm not alright," he told her. "It was a very long night."

"Oh, I'm sorry to hear that. Is everything okay?" Shana's act of concern was impressive, even to herself.

"Were you in my house over the weekend?" He bluntly probed her and she found her most innocent face.

"Of course not. Why would I be, and how would I have even gotten in?"

"Felicia found some women's phone numbers and things around our home, and she didn't believe me when I told her that I don't know where they came from."

"So now you're accusing me of putting them there?" Shana's voice ascended with anger.

"I'm not accusing, just asking," he responded. "They don't belong to me so someone else had to have put them there."

"I see, and out of all of your housekeepers, chef and nannies that are constantly in the house, you just assume that it's me."

"You're the only woman that I've had an affair with, Shana."

"I really doubt that," Shana barked with frustration in her voice. "I don't know how you could even accuse me of this, Don. Yes, I'm hurt that you ended our relationship to work on your marriage, but you know that I would never stoop to doing something like this." Her conjured up tears softened the Governor, leaving him guilt-ridden for his accusation. With her back to him, he approached his assistant, consoling her with his hand on her shoulder.

"Shana, I'm sorry. You're right. I know that you wouldn't do that, and I was wrong to accuse you." Don had fallen into her game without hesitation and her plan was coming together perfectly.

"Perhaps this is out of line but I care about you, and it kills me to see you hurting like this," his assistant inserted, in hopes that he would feel her sincerity. She stared into his anguished eyes of blue, addicted to his soul. This was the only man that she had ever loved and she yearned for his affection, his attention. If only he could realize her desperation for him, he would be hers forever, never to stray, never to again feel pain, but only to love.

Don reached out his arms and embraced his former mistress in what was, to her, the most stimulating comfort in the world. She prayed to stay wrapped in his ecstasy for the rest of her days. Shana yearned to make him understand how much she needed him. She was desperate to tell him how much she craved him and how strong her love for him really was. She had to find a way to make him hers. With him vulnerable, it was her time to strike. A swift slip of her hand to the nape of his neck brought his inviting lips to hers and she made sure to assert the soft passion that he could never resist, the one that hungrily pleaded for him. His moan-enhanced kiss spoke of his desire for Shana, too, until, suddenly, he pulled away from her, shamefaced and remorseful.

"I'm sorry," he spoke a soft apology. "I just can't." It was obvious that it was Don's devotion to his wife that had halted their encounter and she was left, unrewarded, yet again.

"What is it about her, Don?" Shana probed, inquisitively. "What is it about Felicia that makes you love her so deeply?" She was desperate for an answer to the question that endlessly burned her. After a long sigh of thought, he spoke with more authenticity than his assistant had ever before heard from him.

"It's her loyalty, her utter devotion to me and to our children." His words held warmth and adoration as they described his wife. Don sounded as if the epiphany had just grasped his attention. "In all that I've put her through, Felicia is still my biggest supporter, always willing to stand in my shadow and lend me the spotlight. She has put her whole life, her career and her dreams, on hold for me," he told Shana, and for a mere second, she smiled at the thought of a love so genuine. If it weren't for her own agenda with the governor, she would feel sorry for his wife.

"Don, I love you, too," she so sweetly professed, taking his hands in hers. "I'm committed to you, too, and I know that somewhere inside of you, you love me." She searched his eyes for it.

"I do care about you, Shana, very much," he replied with a melting gaze into her eyes, "but I don't love you. I love her." His words pierced her like a jagged sword of a thousand ridges. She stood numb as her face burned with rage. Felicia took precedence in the life of her lover and jealousy suffocated her.

"I'm sorry," Don apologized before his assistant retreated to the restroom with a hung head and tormented soul. She stared at her reflection with loathing of herself, ashamed of the person she was while still yearning for the man she loved.

"I have to find a way for us to be together," she told herself in the water splattered mirror on the wall. "He does love me. I can feel it. I just have to make him see the truth. He belongs with me, not her. She isn't right for him. I am his soul mate." Felicia may have been loyal to Don, but Shana knew that she couldn't make him feel alive like she did. He needed a woman who adored him every single day, catering to his every need and savoring him, someone who didn't have children to take away her time with him. He needed her spontaneity that he loved so much and the excitement that so easily aroused him. Even at home, with his wife, Shana felt that their trysts stayed with Don and played in his head. She felt that he still craved her, even if he couldn't admit it. "How can he really be satisfied with her after the excitement he had with me?" She wondered. He and Felicia lived a dull, lifeless marriage. "I'm the one who really stimulates and excites you." She wondered if he thought about her while he was intimate with his wife. She pondered if they were intimate at all and was certain that they wouldn't be after her finding evidence in their home of an affair the previous night. She hoped that it would cause Felicia to divorce him, or at   least   separate   from   him.

Chapter 9

Still in the hospital, Peter Fallon continued to make a slow recovery from his car crash. The news of his awakening from his coma was traveling swiftly through the office, and rumor had it that he was even beginning to speak a few brief words every now and then.

"I can't allow him to recover and talk about the crash," Shana told herself in a panic. He could ruin her with only a few words.

In the middle of a lengthy and faintly lit corridor of sterile white, Peter lay in a darkened room of silence where the only sound was the monotone beeping of the machines, strategically positioned around his bed. His eyes were peacefully closed on his pale face, and Shana glared down at him in comfort of his misery.

"Well, it looks like you got what you deserved," she spoke softly to him. "I warned you not to get in my way but you just wouldn't listen. Now here you are, defenseless and meek, yet still managing to intrude in my life, and we both know that I can't allow that, Peter." She wondered if he heard her words as they so effortlessly drifted from her vengeful lips. He lay emotionless, his eyes never fluttering, his lips never parting. With a deep sigh of pity, Shana uttered her final words to him. "I don't know why you've forced this," and with his blanket in her hands, she slowly stole his breath, smirking with divine satisfaction.

"Hello," a rising shadow behind her suspiciously greeted forcing the abrupt halt to her amusing plot.

"He may need an extra blanket," Shana sweetly manipulated, pretending to cover him while her heart raced. "He felt a bit cold." She was jolted by the nurse's sudden invasion.

"I don't believe I've seen you here before," the petite brunette mentioned. "Are you a friend of Mr. Fallon's?" Frantically, she searched her mind for a brilliant response.

"Is it really any of your business?" is what Shana was tempted to say. "Governor Tatum's wife, Felicia," she sneered with a proud grin as the young nurse peered at her with confused eyes. "Well, I must be going," his mistress added. "Nice meeting you." She hurried to the elevator with a snicker, realizing how wonderful it sounded to refer to herself as the governor's wife.

Shana's plan to rid herself of Peter Fallon had failed. He was merely a snag in her grand plan to make Don her husband, yet still a hazardous obstacle that was imperative to remove. With the creation of a suspicious nurse, the idea of returning to Peter's hospital room was preposterous. She needed a new plan.

Late that night, Shana returned to her office on a mission. In the darkened quarters of the governor, with only the faded blue light of his computer, she began typing an email, her trained fingers freely flowing through the keys in creation of her message to the local television station.

I write this confession to you with grief in my heart and guilt in my soul. As the governor of this fine state, I feel that honesty is my sworn duty to the residents of Indiana and, therefore, I must, reluctantly and apologetically, admit to a recent affair with a woman other than my wife.

For her sake and that of my family, I elect to keep the identity of my mistress concealed, as I feel it to be a profound detriment to all involved, so I would ask that you relay this information delicately.

As she leaned back in the Governor's gently rocking leather chair, carefully reviewing her words, Shana nodded with a smile of fulfillment.

"That will teach you not to play with the emotions of a woman who loves you," Shana told the absentee.

The admission of the Governor's affair was breaking news the following morning. Every television station and newspaper in the state was reporting the scandal, leaving the bewildered residents questioning who the mystery woman was as the frenzy of reporters outside of the building were bluntly warned to vacate the property. Governor Tatum, who was so adored and trusted, had rapidly become just another adulterous criminal in the political world, and everyone around him had questions that demanded answers. The office had filled itself with assumptions and accusations, and no one spoke of anything else. Shana was satiated with laughter that she didn't dare reveal as she casually made her way to Johanna's desk.

"This is preposterous!" Shana exclaimed in an imperfect element of surprise. "Do you hear what is being reported?"

With a distrustful stare of aversion from the woman who snubbed her, Mrs. Tatum's assistant nodded. "I think there's truth to it, too."

"You don't think it's someone here, in the office, do you?" Shana tried desperately to divert any suspicion away from her as the rumors flurried into a whirlwind.

"I seriously doubt it," she answered snidely. "He has women all over the place." Johanna's bold statement threw Shana into an immediate gasp for air as she felt her face fall numb. Don had other women? She wasn't his only mistress? So long she had spent, convinced that he risked his marriage out of unwavering love for her, only to hear that there were others.

"Pull yourself together," she told herself as her aching heart worsened. "Stay calm. Don't give yourself away. I wasn't aware of any of that," Shana replied with an attempt at appearing not to care, "but it's his personal business and I promise to keep that confidential," she assured Johanna.

She casually found her way back to her desk, awaiting Don's arrival but, still, there was no sign of him in the office.

"Excuse me, Shana", one of his aides approached. "The Governor called and asked me to relay to you that he will be working from his home today. Due to the news reports, he and I will be there putting together a press conference for this afternoon. Damage control." She snickered deviously.

"Of course, I understand," she nodded. "I will reschedule today's appointments."

"Great, and if anyone asks, just tell them that he is doing business from home today and is requesting no interruptions."

"Absolutely, I'll take care of it," she replied with a pleasant smile, which quickly turned to a wide grin as he walked away. Her plan was working flawlessly.

"We are just moments away from Indiana Governor, Don Tatum's press conference, when he is expected to address allegations of an affair with an unidentified woman," the news anchor announced on the television. His office staff gathered, intent on hearing his explanation, as whispers invaded the silence. Shana was more curious than anyone, and she couldn't wait to hear his response to the scandal. It wasn't an accusation that could be easily explained. The governor, hesitantly, stepped to the mass of microphones and cameras with a dim expression.

"Today, I would like to address allegations that have been made regarding my having an inappropriate relationship with a woman other than my wife," he began with the devoted Felicia at his side. Her face spoke of a distraught child, grieving and lost. "I want the people of this great state to know that this hurtful accusation is entirely false and is being thoroughly investigated. It is unfortunate that someone has made such a claim, and my hope is that the issue can be resolved quickly, without undue invasion of my mission as your governor."

"Is there any indication of who made this claim, Governor?" A reporter probed. Shana gasped in silence, hoping that she wasn't a suspect.

"To the best of my knowledge, it is an anonymous person at this time," Don answered, and she was able to relax.

"Governor, is there any reason that someone might make this allegation?" Another yelled out to him.

"There is no specific reason that I'm aware of," the governor responded, "other than the possibility of plaguing my election campaign."

Shana watched in disbelief over his ability to so easily deceive his supporters with lies while his wife stood, loyally, by him. His lack of responsibility astounded her. How could he not admit to his relationship with her, she wondered.

How could he pretend that she meant nothing to him, like she never mattered? She wondered how his wife could support his story, given the evidence that she, herself, had against him. Nothing that Shana did won Don back. Her plans were masterfully tailored to shatter his perfect marriage and lead him back into her arms but none of her attempts were successful, and she pondered what element it was that made their marriage so indestructible. She had to find a way to get him back.

The scandal surrounding the governor appeared to be the primary topic of conversation throughout his office and amidst the town, and the gossipers were seemingly equally divided on their views. Some spoke of their shock and disappointment of their beloved Don Tatum while others weren't at all staggered.

"All politicians have mistresses," they said. "I'm just surprised that he was able to hide it this long." Even among their contrasted opinions, the lingering question on everyone's tongue was who the mystery woman was. Shana listened carefully to the whispers around her to ensure that she wasn't suspected.

In the hours that followed the governor's press conference, she was approached by several of her meddling coworkers, all casually attempting to pump her for any possible information as if she was clueless to their intentions.

"You didn't know anything about this, you know, being his assistant and all?" One particularly nosy woman in her fifties probed. "I mean, usually the secretaries get wind of this sort of thing."

"No, I had no idea at all," Shana responded. "I'm just as shocked as everyone else."

"It's appalling," the woman remarked. "I hope that his poor wife takes everything that he has." It wouldn't matter to Shana if that were the case. All she wanted was the man.

"Well, she appears to be standing by him."

"Maybe so," the employee replied, "but his reputation is already ruined."

In Shana's apartment that evening, the news channels replayed Don's comments during his news conference, along with a panel of political analysts, each one speculating on the future of the governor's reign.

"My view is that impeachment or his resignation could be a viable option at this point," one panelist opined. "People need to feel like their governor is sincere and I don't think that most will excuse his behavior."

"We don't even have proof that he's guilty of adultery," another rebutted. "This is merely an accusation from someone who has still not even come forward. There's no real substantiation at this juncture and so, I don't think that we'll see a resignation or grounds for impeachment. There's no validity for it."

"Look what you've caused, Don," Shana said to herself, observing the tie-clad men on television. "Not only have you blemished your perfect reputation, but now you're denying that our affair even happened." Shana felt rejected and she refused to allow it. He had to pay for what he had done to her, she thought. She wasn't about to let him toss her aside, as if she was garbage, just to save his flawless reputation. If he wouldn't acknowledge her like she felt she deserved, then she would further increase the turmoil in his life. "When I'm finished, we'll just see who the important one is in your life," she said. First though, she still had Peter Fallon to deal with.

"Hello, Peter," Shana greeted him when she brazenly entered his room, even after she swore she wouldn't return. He lay, groggily, awake and peering suspiciously at her. "How are you feeling?" Peter struggled to speak in his weakened state. "It's okay," she told him. "You don't have to answer that because well, frankly, I'm just making conversation anyway. I snuck you in a milkshake, you know, the kind we used to stop for, on occasion, after our rendezvous." Holding the straw to his flaky lips, she offered him a sip of the vanilla goodness that he so loved. He was fragile, hardly able to sit up in the hospital bed as he sipped her poisonous blend. "I've missed you, Peter," she remarked, "and you know, I've been here quite frequently to visit you. That must have been a terrible crash." He continued to sip, ever so slowly, as she slipped a cocktail of crushed pills in his mouth. Her plan to rid herself of him wouldn't be foiled again. "I think I'm actually going to miss you," she spoke with a sarcastic snarl. "It's just too bad that your life was cut so short." Drugged and barely conscious, his fragile face looked as if he had no real recognition of her. She glared at her defenseless victim with a widening

97

grin of satisfaction. "Goodbye, Peter. See you in hell," she told him before making an inconspicuous exit. She strutted through the hospital parking lot in her skirt and heels, tossing the empty foam cup in a nearby dumpster. "Rest in peace, Peter Fallon," she said with a smirk on the way back to her car.

Chapter 10

Shana arrived back at her apartment to find Don waiting for her in the parking lot. She was thrilled to see him. Surely, he'd been missing her, she thought.

"Well, hello," she greeted him. "I knew you'd be back sooner or later."

"We need to talk." His firm tone matched the seriousness on his face.

"Yes, of course," she replied with a smile. "I have something exciting to tell you." He followed her into her apartment and sat down in the undersized living room. "Can I get you a drink? I'm sure that you're probably needing one after today."

"No, Shana, please, sit down," he said. She sat next to him on the couch.

"I came to tell you, in person, that we can't work together anymore," he uttered with an unwavering face. His words left her in a stunned silence. "Believe me when I say that, professionally, you've done a great job as my assistant and, therefore, my intention is not to eject you from my office. I will ensure that you have an equal position in the building."

She was flabbergasted by his sudden decision. "Listen, Don, I realize that you have a lot going on right now because of this scandal, but is this really necessary? I mean, no one knows about our relationship and this will inflict suspicion, don't you think?"

"It's not a relationship, Shana, and it's not about that. I just think that, given the circumstances, I need an assistant who is . . ."

"Who is what, older and less attractive?" She intervened. "You're afraid of what people will say because you have a young, attractive assistant?"

"I can't afford any further suspicion, Shana," he responded. "It's just not appropriate, given our past, and you, yourself, have made it quite clear that you have strong feelings for me." She couldn't believe his audacity.

"I realize that you have to be cautious, Don, but it isn't exactly fair for me to pay for the allegations against you," she told him. "I beg you to reconsider your decision, well, that is, unless you think I'm the one who made those accusations." His apprehensive glare let her know that it was true. "Wait a minute," she said. "You do, don't you? You think it was me."

"I don't know who it was," Don responded, and though it may have been her guilt-tainted soul, she was sure that he was lying. "The point here is that we can't work together anymore."

"I would only be hurting myself to do something like that," Shana told him, "because I'm pregnant." Her announcement had come from nowhere and had been invented just a second before, created from pure desperation in an attempt to retain a connection to her lover.

The governor's face grew ashen as hysteria invaded him. He was nauseated with distress and for a mere second, she was repentant for her untruth but, even so, it was necessary. She needed to hold on to the man that she loved and there was nothing that she wouldn't do to keep him. Don was a family man. He was devoted to his children and, to Shana, it was a surefire way to regain her lover's loyalty.

"You're pregnant? Are you sure?" He was dumbstruck by her sudden announcement, stumbling for words and, seemingly, breathing erratically.

"Yes, I'm sure and, before you ask, it is yours and I'm keeping the baby." If only her fabrication was the truth, she thought. It was what she had yearned for each time that she and Don had made love, and as far as he knew, it had happened.

"I thought we were protected," he responded in a profuse panic, frantically searching himself for a plan.

"I thought so, too, but maybe it's just meant to be," Shana told him. "Would it be so bad to have a child, conceived from love?"

"You just don't get it," he scowled with disappointment in the midst of his nightmare. "I already have a family, Shana, and this is going to tear them apart, not to mention destroying my position as governor." She was revolted to hear that his concern was his reputation rather than the baby that he thought they would be having. It was as if he didn't care at all. His status meant more to him than their family.

"I can't believe you!" She growled. "This baby, our baby, means nothing to you?" Don's eyes softened as he gradually calmed his anxiety.

"Of course it does," he replied genuinely. "You know how important my children are to me. I will be there for this one, too, but you have to promise me that you'll keep this quiet until I can prepare my family."

"Okay, I understand," she reluctantly agreed, "but only if I keep my job as your assistant. Besides, how will it look if you suddenly dismiss me during this scandal?"

"I just don't think that's a good idea, Shana."

"Let me be blunt with you, Don", she replied. "If I lose my position, you lose your pristine reputation. Consider it my sense of security that our child has its father." The governor took a deep breath to conjure his patience.

"I won't allow you to blackmail me."

"Maybe I should handle this with your wife since you seem so uncooperative," she delivered her ultimatum with raised eyebrows. The fury housed in his eyes was clear.

"Damn it, Shana!" He huffed. "I'm suffocating! My whole world is crumbling around me." Tears flooded Don's eyes as he paced the floor of her living room, assumingly wishing his catastrophe away. She arose and took him gently by the arm.

"Don, your political status, your income, your reputation – none of it matters to me," she told him softly, staring into his helpless eyes. "You're the man I love and I'm here for you, no matter what. I want us to be a family."

The anguished governor sobbed, uncontrollably, as his assistant held him, tightly, in her arms. "I just don't know what to do," he told her. "I'm losing control."

"I'm not going to make it harder on you," Shana consoled him, rubbing his back and as their eyes connected, she kissed him, softly, and he responded. The familiar rapture, once again, cradled her and in his arms is where she felt her place in the world was. The emotion only reinforced her desperate need for him in her life. It wasn't possible to let him go when the feeling that they were meant for each other overwhelmed her. He pulled her closer as their lips were meshed in a starving passion and, soon, they were entwined within her satin sheets, the feel of his skin touching hers electrifying her soul. Once again, he was hers, even if just for the moment. His affection meant that he still needed her, too.

As she lay in her lover's arms, Don caressed her barren womb. "What should we name it?" He remarked, affectionately.

Shana beamed with delight at his acceptance of having a child with her and she yearned to make it happen. Every previous attempt at conceiving a baby with him had failed but she held onto the hope that this time was different. Having Don's child, she felt, would guarantee her a permanent place in his life.

"Maybe Ashley or Cody?" She replied to the governor's question.

"Those are nice," he responded, "or perhaps Julia or Joseph."

For Shana, the moment was perfect. She lay, wrapped in the embrace of the man of her dreams, thankful for the security of his arms that comforted her as the two of them discussed their future. The life she dreamed of danced in her head – exchanging their vows in a stunning gown of white before hundreds, evenings cuddled together on the sofa and the vision of sun-kissed picnics with the two children that she wished for. Shana was desperate to create that world with Don. In her fantasy, the governor belonged to her. The mere thought of him with anyone else was intolerable to her.

"I love you, Don," she professed. "I mean, I know that we never planned for any of this to happen between us but it did, and I feel like it's all just meant to be. I dream of you being mine, building a life together, a family. No one can possibly love you like I do," and as she poured out her soul, she heard his snore. She glanced at him to find him asleep. With a deep sigh of discontent, she snuggled tightly against him and closed her eyes, unable to get enough of his aura.

Two hours later, Shana was jarred awake by Don's frantic leap out of her bed. "Oh God, it's eleven o'clock! I fell asleep!"

"It's okay, you . . ."

"No, it's not okay," he interrupted. "Felicia is going to have my head!" He scurried around the darkened room, racing in search for his clothes. "I'm sorry, I have to go," Don said, and he rushed out the door. Shana lay, overcome with aggravation over his wife's precedence over her.

"You always run right back to her," she commented to herself. "It won't be this way for much longer, though. Our baby will be his priority now." She relished the idea of a family with her lover. Clearly, it was just a matter of time before Don was hers, only hers, forever, she thought.

The following morning, Shana poured a cup of coffee and turned on the news on her television. She lit the fireplace to combat the chill in her apartment and sat in the recliner with her favorite blanket.

"If Don was here right now, I would be cooking him breakfast and snuggling to keep warm," she told herself, imagining the two enrapt in an embrace. Her mind fell into an image of him in his robe, approaching her from behind as she prepared his breakfast and wrapping them both in a blanketed cuddle while happily kissing her neck.

"Good morning, beautiful," he greeted in her fantasy.

When she found her reality, once again, Shana wondered what he was doing at that moment. She pictured him at the kitchen table with his coffee, reading the newspaper while his kids watched cartoons in the living room. It was the life that she dreamed of with the governor.

"In other news today, Peter Fallon, a top Aide to Governor Don Tatum, has died," the blond-haired anchor announced on television. Shana grabbed the remote control and turned up the volume. "He had been in the hospital since July, recovering from a car crash that left him critically injured. Hospital officials say that he succumbed to his injuries yesterday afternoon." Relief bred itself within her when it was reported that Peter's death was the result of his injuries. No one seemed to suspect foul play and she was safe. A part of her empathized with Peter's family over their sorrow. After all, it wasn't his wife and children who had forced her hand. Only he had been her obstacle. Guilt drifted in as she thought of their penalty.

"No," she told herself, "Peter caused this, not me and I won't feel guilty for it."

Shana had more important things to worry about, and her primary concern was winning over Don Tatum. Her contention of pregnancy had proven a good start but she was forced into the future. In just a few months, she would have to begin looking the part in order to see it through. Furthermore, Don would eventually expect a baby. She had some planning to do.

Chapter 11

Peter's funeral was two days later and seemingly every person in town crammed the building to pay their respects. It was clear to Shana that she had no place there, among those who respected him, but she feared that not attending would display her guilt.

Hesitantly, she approached the casket for a final glance of her pale-faced victim, and her skin crawled with anxiety because of her crime. Staring down at the lifeless man haunted her, as if he would spring up to attack her in an instant. "Why did you have to get in my way?" Shana asked him in silence, almost remorseful of his murder.

His funeral service was a gloomy array of inconsolable mourners and speakers eulogizing the memory of him as a respectable and loving man, never knowing his darker side, and Shana wondered why she never saw it in him. The two of them had never surpassed the sexual side for her to know him any differently, and she wished that things had been different. From afar, she eyed Peter's wife, sorrowfully wiping away her tears in the front pew, forced to bid farewell to the only man she had ever loved, and Shana sympathized with her. She knew life without a man to love. Don approached the podium to speak.

"Peter Fallon was not only a respected colleague of mine but also a loyal friend," he began and, as he spoke, Shana gazed at him with doting eyes, hanging tightly to his every word. She observed his demeanor, right down to the movement of his satin lips, and she swore that with each passing day, her adoration for him was even more amplified. The signature of death reiterated the importance of making the governor hers. It restated that life was just too short to simply wait on her dreams to happen. She needed to make them happen. At the funeral's finale, Shana reluctantly converged on Peter's wife.

"Mrs. Fallon, I want to offer my condolences to your family." The widow led her outside and, with a deep breath, she began.

"I know about you and Peter." Shana's eyes widened while her breath quivered with nervousness and shame. "I know about the affair." She peered calmly at the ground before returning her focus to the eyes of her late husband's mistress. "At first, I didn't believe it, but I guess in my heart, I knew it was true," she confessed. Shana wanted, desperately, to explain to her that their affair was never what she wanted.

"Mrs. Fallon, I . . ."

"Don't," the woman interrupted with her hand halting Shana's response. "I called you out here to give you this." She presented a rectangle box. She glared at Peter's wife with perplexed vision. "He must have been on his way to see you when he crashed. I know that it's for you because I mistakenly opened it." It was an envelope addressed as *My Darling*. Shana was mystified and speechless with disbelief in the discomforting moment. "If nothing else, I suppose he died happy," Peter's widow concluded with a face full of anguish and with her head hung, she walked sadly away.

Shana was at a loss of words, stunned over what had just occurred and, as much as she battled it, her conscience controlled her. In the car, she opened Peter's letter to her.

My Dearest Shana, it read. *You changed my life the moment I met you. Never have I felt more vivacious than with you in my world. Our time together, for me, has been nothing short of magical. It's been misery coming to terms with you loving someone other than me but I want you to be happy and so this is my parting gift. Always know in your heart that you are worthy of the best. Peter*

Shana was both stunned and flattered by Peter's words. She was unaware that she had triggered such emotions within the man that she had dubbed an egotistical womanizer, who was

109

blackmailing her into his own sexual pleasures. His letter lent her a different story, the account of unintentional love, about a person so desperately in need of her that he did whatever was necessary to keep his flame burning. Shana realized that he wasn't much different from her after all. Not unlike her, his desperation for another overruled his judgment. Suddenly, she could identify with Peter and even discovered an appreciation for him.

Slowly, she opened the velvet box to expose the most exquisite necklace of diamonds that her eyes had ever descended upon. She stared, breathlessly, at her luxurious gift of elegance, convinced that her eyes were fooling her. The necklace had surely cost a fortune which left her perplexed as to why Peter's wife had given it to her rather than keeping it for herself.

A tap on her car window nearly jolted Shana from her seat. The hunched over governor stood, motioning for her to roll down the window as she breathed a sigh of relief to calm her rapidly pulsating heart.

"Are you trying to give me a heart attack?" She ribbed him.

"I'm sorry, I just . . ." he explained until he spotted the jewelry box. "What is that?"

"It's just a piece of jewelry that I let someone borrow a while back," she responded, hardly with any thought. "She returned it today." With a puzzled expression, he blew it off and returned to his reason for approaching her.

"I just wanted to thank you for coming today," Don sincerely spoke. "I know that Peter really thought a lot of you." Shana battled a gasp of uneasiness. Did Don know more than she thought he did? How much had Peter told him? She pondered.

"I had a lot of respect for him also," she replied with an innocuous smile.

"Felicia and the kids are in the car so I have to go."

"Will I see you later?" Shana hoped for some time alone with her lover.

"Tonight isn't good for me. Sorry," he replied, scurrying away with a friendly wave. His response was the same familiar answer that she had always given Peter to rid herself of him and she knew it well. His mistress watched with disappointment as the man she loved dutifully left with his family. She resented his wife for having Don's devotion, the one thing that she desired most in the world.

In her apartment, Shana spent the weekend sewing form-fitting rubber pads of varying sizes, to strap to her stomach through her pregnancy plot. Her co-workers and, especially Don, would be touching her stomach throughout the months to come so she needed something as realistic as possible. In front of her full length bedroom mirror, she examined her image in each of the four sizes, analyzing every detail – size, feel, proportion – and she was ecstatically proud of her creations.

The days that followed in the governor's office were fueled with whispered theories, as had become customary in the previous weeks, amidst all of the extraordinary occurrences. The employees spoke of Peter's peculiar death while rumors of Don's alleged affair also lingered. Shana didn't appear to be suspected in either situation from the parts that she overheard. She, alone, held the answers that everyone around her searched for. Her vast efforts to conceal her involvement permeated her into the confidential conversations of her peers.

"Have you heard anything else yet?" She probed to turn their suspicions away from her.

There had been a vacancy in Don's office for two days and his only contact was a brief business call or two to check in. His blatant lack of attention only intensified her dissatisfaction. To his knowledge, Shana was in a fragile stage of pregnancy with his child and his neglect infuriated her. Where was his loyalty and concern, she wondered.

"We need to talk," she had mentioned during one of the governor's short-lived phone calls.

"Okay, but not right now," was his response, a common dismissal that only aggravated her further.

After three days of being insolently evaded by her lover, Shana refused to be ignored any longer. That evening, she dialed his phone number, with vigilance, in demand of his attention, and she would accept nothing less.

"Why haven't you called me back, Don?" She interrogated when he answered his cell phone.

"Hi, yes, um, could we please discuss this issue tomorrow when I'm in the office?" He spoke in a professional manner in an obvious attempt to obscure her from his family.

"No, we can't discuss this tomorrow," Shana growled with ferocity. "You're not going to just toss me aside. I'm the mother of your child."

"I do realize that, and may I please call you back very shortly?" Don pleaded. "This isn't a good time." His tone announced Felicia's presence.

"Fine, but if I haven't heard back from you within the hour, I'm calling again and next time, it will be on your house phone to talk to your wife." She was enraged at Don's attempt to avoid her as if she was of no priority to him, and she refused to allow it.

In fear that Shana would follow through with her threat, the governor returned her phone call a half hour later, when he was able to escape his family.

"Listen, I understand your situation, but you just can't call me at home," he told his mistress.

"My situation?" She couldn't believe his audacity. "This is our situation, Don, whether you like it or not and frankly, I don't appreciate being shoved in the corner while you gratify your wife. You haven't even told her yet, have you?" The long sigh on the phone answered her question.

"I just need a little more time, Shana," he explained. "This is a very delicate issue and I have to tell her the right way."

"You know, I don't need your excuses. I'll maintain my silence but only as long as you maintain your loyalty to me. That means daily phone calls, frequent visits and genuine concern for me and this baby." She spewed her demands with fierce gravity. The governor was conquered. His mistress had put her terms out to him and if he didn't comply, his life, as he knew it, would be ruined in an instant. Don had no choice but to do exactly as Shana commanded. He was entirely at her mercy if he wanted to keep their affair undetected. The newfound empowerment that Shana felt was insurmountable. Finally, she had her lover exactly where she wanted him, and she planned to blackmail him back into her arms for good. As long as she held the upper hand, she could get nearly whatever she wanted out of him and it felt wonderful. Shana was exuberant with control.

Over the few weeks that followed, the governor was submissive to his assistant's every whim. He responded whenever he was summoned by her, and he played the part of the doting boyfriend that she insisted on having. He brought her dinner, cuddled with her in front of the television and made love to her just as if he was her husband. Don quickly found himself acting the husband of two families and it weighed heavily on him. Felicia's suspicions had intensified with his every excuse for his additional time away from their family, and exhaustion overwhelmed him as he struggled to accommodate both mothers of his children. Even the governor's political career began to suffer in his juggling act and his aides pressured him over his lack of concentration.

"We need to focus on your upcoming debate, Governor," his top aide asserted. "There are a lot of issues on the table for this election, and your opponent appears extremely confident."

"I'm on top of it and prepared," Don assured him. "Things have just been crazy lately but I'm focused."

"We have to be because Gary Dunrite is on top of his game and anxious to fill your seat as governor, and I won't be at all surprised if he dredges up the affair scandal all over again, just to drag you through the mud," the governor's aide remarked. "He plays dirty."

"I'll be ready," the governor insisted.

"Shana, we have to figure something else out here," Don asserted during his next visit. "This is all getting to be too much on me and now, Felicia suspects that the affair is true." He took a deep breath and continued. "I have to start spending a little more time at home and, with the election so close, I can't have any more uncertainties on me." His mistress glared defiantly at him with lasers aimed to fire.

"Let me get this straight," she said. "You caused this whole situation by having an affair and, now that you're having trouble juggling it all, I'm the one, yet again, that is being forced to suffer your absence?"

"Shana, please . . ."

"No, don't," she said with a spring from the couch. "I've always been forced to the bottom of your priorities and I won't be anymore. I don't know how you're going to spread yourself out but it needs to be clear that, this time, it won't be me left alone. If Felicia has such a problem with you being gone so much, then maybe it's time for you to tell her the truth."

"I just can't yet," he replied, shaking his lowered head in dismay.

"When are you going to tell her, Don, when the baby is born? She needs to know because she's going to find out sooner or later," Shana responded. "Are you afraid of losing her, or the election?"

"I'm afraid of losing my children," he replied, mournfully but she couldn't empathize with him any longer. It was time for Don to make a decision and, with the power that she still maintained over him, Shana was sure that she would be his selection, especially since it was unlikely that his wife would stay with him after he confessed to her. "You don't understand what this is doing to me."

"And I don't think you understand what it's doing to me," she rebutted with folded arms and an intent glare. "It's time for you to make a decision." He stared at the floor in confusion, pondering his choice. The governor's loyalty was with his wife and children, but he was well aware that Shana could destroy him. Still, he could only choose one. After several minutes with his head in his hands, obviously pondering his future and what was the best option for everyone involved, Don looked up at her with wounded eyes.

"I'm going to tell Felicia," he responded with desolation, "but please, just give me until after the debate, okay? Just give me that time."

With a deep breath of reluctance, Shana agreed. Once again, it was he who was the victim,

116

the one to be sympathized with, and she was left consoling him.

Shana wondered what Felicia's reaction would be when she was finally told of her husband's infidelity. Would she leave, or stand by him like so many other political wives did? Surely, she wouldn't accept another woman's child in the fairytale life that she had created, Shana thought. Perhaps Felicia would see no other option but to let Don go. After all, they didn't have to be married for him to remain a good father to their children, she told herself.

She closed her eyes and imagined her future with the man that she loved, cuddled on the couch together with his children and theirs, together, as a happy family. The fairytale, then, would be hers.

Chapter 12

Shana squeezed into the first pregnancy suit that she'd tailored to look the part of a woman who was five months along. She stared at her moderately swollen midsection in the mirror, wishing that her pregnancy was authentic and yearning for a baby with Don. She stood before the mirror, gently stroking her expanded stomach and, as she did, it all became real. To her, it wasn't a suit but more the indication of what was to be – a child made of Don and her. More than the appearance was the overwhelming feeling that dwelled within her, the comfort that she and Don would soon be a family, just as she had always dreamed of.

"What am I going to tell everyone at the office if they notice?" She pondered. Since she had never mentioned having a man in her life to any of her peers, some would, surely, ask about the father. They would look at her with disdain if she claimed a one night stand, and it was doubtful that anyone would believe that she used a sperm donor since she had never expressed a desire for a baby. She certainly couldn't admit her claim that it was the governor's child to her co-workers. Her only option was to claim an accidental pregnancy from brief relationship and, though she felt that they might still scorn her, it was the most plausible story.

The debate was over and Don still hadn't told his wife about Shana and the baby like he had vowed to do. His excuses of being too busy were quickly growing old and Shana threatened to tell his secret.

"Please, I just need a little more time," he pleaded. "Things are so crazy right now but I promise to tell her soon. Just give another week." Reluctantly, she acquiesced.

With the election drawing near, the governor's office bustled in preparation. Don hibernated behind closed doors with his aides, and Shana found it nearly impossible to divert his attention. He refused all interruptions except those from his wife who, it appeared, intervened several times that day for one insignificant reason or another. Shana found herself enraged that, once again, Felicia Tatum held a higher priority than her, despite Don's baby that he thought that she was carrying. Because she wasn't on his list of priorities, Shana was sure that he still hadn't even told his family about the pregnancy yet. It was the last straw for her. If Don wouldn't grant her his attention and respect that she felt she deserved, then she was prepared to take matters into her own hands.

As she neared the exit for her weekly visit to the campaign headquarters, Shana was stopped by Felicia's assistant, Johanna.

"I'm glad I caught you before you left," she commented nearly breathless from her sprint. "Could you take these pins and flyers with you?"

"Oh, of course," Shana replied with a friendly smile.

"By the way, I don't mean to pry, but is there something you haven't told us?" Her curious eyes gestured to her co-worker's swollen womb. She snickered with apprehension.

"Well, I've been discreet about it, you know, wearing baggy clothes and everything, because I didn't want to jinx it so early on." She prepped herself for the swath of questions about to ensue but, to her surprise, all that followed was a mere congratulations and Shana was relieved not to have to explain. Still, she knew that her news would quickly spread through the office and it was sure to be the new topic of gossip.

The women at the campaign headquarters had snubbed Shana since she left them to work in Don's office and, though they were suspicious of hers and the governor's relationship, none could ever prove anything other than professionalism between them. Even so, she was a plague to them, and their unspoken distaste for her was always clear as it seemed a struggle for them just to be civil to her.

"Whoa, I've never noticed that you're pregnant," one woman snootily chirped during Shana's visit. "I didn't realize that you're married." Her sarcasm was an obvious intention to degrade her character. Shana was incensed but determined to maintain her civility.

"I'm not married, actually, but the pregnancy was planned with a very special man," she responded with as much politeness as she could muster and, as the middle-aged woman eyed her with confusion, Shana walked away in triumph. "That should give them something to talk about for a while," she thought to herself. From the campaign office, she drove to the governor's mansion with fortitude in her heart and purpose in her mind.

"Shana, hello," Felicia greeted her with astounded eyes at their personal quarters. "Come in." The women sat in the formal living room near the soothing flame in the exquisite stone fireplace, sipping hot tea. The governor's assistant examined her immaculate competition, her posh blue business suit and matching jewels and her hair swept so gently up, showcasing her porcelain face.

"I'm sorry to bother you, Mrs. Tatum, but there's something important that I need to speak with you about." She peered at her adversary, almost empathetic to her feelings. In other circumstances, the pair could potentially be friends, but she was Shana's competition, the obstacle that stood between her and the only man she loved and, for that reason, she needed to be merciless. There was just no place for sympathy. "There's no easy way to say this so excuse me for being so direct,"

121

she explained. Concern fell upon Felicia's face as she listened intently. "I've been having an affair with your husband and I'm carrying his baby." Her confession delighted her as she boasted about their fling. Shana could almost see the very breath abscond from her lover's wife. She sat, speechless and spellbound, in a struggle to absorb the mistress's confession. Her intense anguish displayed itself, explicitly, in her eyes.

"How long has this been going on?" She finally uttered in a soft and broken tone, too stunned to shed even a single tear while knowing it was true.

"It's been several months," Shana answered wryly, almost proud of her victory. In her mind, the best woman had won Don's affection and she found it satisfying to have destroyed Felicia's perfect world. "He was supposed to tell you. We felt that you needed to know." Felicia glared at her husband's mistress, distrustfully, with the eyes of a wounded child.

"Are you in love with him?" She probed. Shana stared back at the governor's wife a stimulating fulfillment, about to add to her abuse.

"Don and I are in love with each other. I'm sorry that it had to come out this way, Mrs. Tatum, but we are going to be together. We're going to be a family." The grief of his wife quickly evolved to rage and the determination to hold onto her husband, the man that she'd built her life around for so many years.

"In case you haven't noticed, he already has a family, Shana, and you should know that I don't intend to let you intervene." Her eyes were heartless swords that pierced her. "I think you should leave now."

"Of course," she replied, politely, and made her way to the door. "You know, our children will be siblings so it would be best if we could, somehow, work this out."

"Just get out of my house," the heartbroken victim demanded, slamming the door as her aggressor strutted away.

Shana was proud of the turmoil that she had just created in Don's marriage. She felt it the necessary nudge that he needed to begin a new relationship with her and, in her heart, she was certain of his gratitude for the devotion to him that she had shown in confronting his wife. The governor's call to her cell phone told her that he had already spoken to Felicia.

"What the hell did you do?" He yelled when she answered. "You told my wife?"

His irritation left Shana baffled. "I did it because you couldn't, and she needed to know."

"She didn't need to hear it from you, Shana. We agreed that I would tell her but you decided, on your own, to go ahead and ruin my life now, didn't you?" His exasperation caught her by surprise and her heart pounded wildly within her.

"Don, calm down," his mistress calmly replied, mystified by his fury. She couldn't understand his disapproval of her decision. After all, she had done it to make it easier for him. "I did it to help you. I did it for us."

"No, you did it solely for your own self-satisfaction and to hurt the people I love," he scowled. "Do you even fathom what you've just caused? I can't believe that you did this to me!"

"You don't love me?" Shana responded to his comments.

"Are you stupid? I never loved you. You were just there, Shana. I love my wife and now, thanks to you, my life is destroyed," he shrieked. "You stay away from my family and from me!"

She couldn't believe what she was hearing. His words, newly honed daggers, repeatedly impaling her chest. She had never before felt so betrayed and degraded. His icy criticisms dubbed her trash and she refused to accept his cruelty. She wouldn't play second to Felicia, even if she was Don's wife. Shana was accustomed to getting what she wanted, and she was determined to be with the man that she loved at any cost.

"Please, let's talk about this," she pleaded with her lover.

"No, I'm finished talking to you," he insisted. "This is done!"

"You said we'd be together," she sobbed. "We're supposed to be a family."

"I have a family, Shana, and you're no part of it. Stay away from us or I'll have you arrested." She was left broken when he abruptly hung up on her.

"How dare he treat me like this!" She scowled. "Who does he think he is, tossing me aside like I'm nothing?" She huffed with gritted teeth through her tears. "He might think this is over but he's dead wrong." As far as she was concerned, it was far from over. She refused to give up on the only person that she had in the world.

With Don infuriated, Shana thought it best not to return to the office that day. Her empowering ability to jeopardize the election granted her the upper hand, even in spite of his malice. The last thing that the governor wanted was another scandal while he was campaigning for votes. His mistress clearly held his career in her hands and knowing that exhilarated her. Shana was positive that he would crawl back to her, apologetically, once he realized the damage that she could bestow on him. Besides, she thought, she and Don were meant for each other. She was convinced of it.

Chapter 13

Shana arrived at the office the following morning to find the governor awaiting her.

"Come into my office," he commanded her, frigidly, and she followed him in, closing the door behind them. "Don't bother sitting down. This will only take a minute." He began. "I want you to clear out your desk and leave, promptly." Her pulsating heart fell swiftly to her stomach as she listened to him expel her from his life.

"You're firing me?" She asked as if his demand hadn't already confirmed it.

"You're a detriment, not only to me and my family but also to this election and, most of all, to yourself," the governor explained with as much patience as he could gather amidst his fury, his face bitter as he glared at her distressed eyes.

"Don, I'm sorry for telling Felicia about us, but I need this job," his assistant pleaded with innocence in her eyes and a grasp on his arms. "Please, don't do this. I'm the mother of your child."

"It's over, Shana," was his response as he firmly released himself from her grip. "That child will be taken care of but you need to leave this office voluntarily, or I'll have no choice but to have you escorted out of the building."

Ferocity overtook her. She was pained by his unemotional lack of compassion, his words spewing poison into her veins, confiscating the life from her. He disintegrated her world, without even an ounce of remorse, and it was the most agonizing distress that she'd ever felt.

"You won't get away with this, Don," she warned. "You think I've caused you trouble before but you haven't seen anything yet!" Shana stormed out of his office, determined to make him pay for the grief that he was causing her.

She drove straight to his opponent's office across town.

"Hello, I need to see Gary Dunrite, please," she requested of the secretary at the front desk.

"Do you have an appointment?" The fifty something year old woman asked with a close examination of her.

"No, ma'am, but I'm sure that he'll want to speak with me. I'm Governor Tatum's secretary." Intrigue consumed her face.

"Let me check with him for you," she replied before disappearing down the hallway.

Shana's eyes drifted around the entrance of the office, acknowledging its rasping antique floors and plastic-cushioned wooden chairs. Shoddy pictures of flowers adorned the pale-colored walls, and she couldn't help but assume that they'd been bought at a yard sale or consignment shop. The office was aged and substandard for a man who was campaigning to be the next governor of Indiana. She had expected plush leather furniture and fine paintings or sculptures.

The secretary reappeared and permitted Shana into Gary's office and, as she made her way down the corridor, she loosened two buttons on her red blouse.

"Hello, Mr. Dunrite, thanks for taking the time to speak with me," she greeted with a congenial smile. His intrigue was, immediately, obvious to her when his fascinated eyes absorbed her.

"Hello, come in." The silver-haired man nearly stumbled over his desk to approach her, infatuated with her appeal. "Please, sit down."

"I'm so sorry to barge in on you like this, Mr. Dunrite. I realize that you're very busy, but I have a proposition for you." Don's opponent perked up in his black leather chair with elevated brows, as though he had just won the lottery, and she could only imagine the perversion reeling through his mind. "All politicians are the same," she told herself in silence. "What if I said that I can guarantee you a win in the election?" The middle-aged man was fascinated, though he exerted every effort to appear unimpressed.

"Well, I can't deny that you've piqued my curiosity," he responded with a slight grin, "but aren't you Governor Tatum's assistant?"

"I was until he let me go this morning," Shana answered with a devious stare that displayed her quest for revenge.

"I see," Gary replied, and her innuendo was clear. "So you can make me the governor but at what cost?"

"Well, since I was let go this morning, I need a job," she told him. The political hopeful appeared impressed with her suave ability to strike a deal.

"I suppose I could use a little more help around here," he smirked, "especially if I win. You're quite self-assured to guarantee my winning the election. Tell me, how do you plan to do that?"

"I was also the governor's mistress," Shana blatantly confessed and her words danced in his delighted ears, "the one that you probably heard about in every media outlet in Indiana."

"Ah, so you're the mystery woman."

"Yes, I am, and I'm carrying his child," the scorned lover added. His face lit up at her admission. The governor's mistress was Gary's jackpot. "Only Don and his wife know, and I told her because he wouldn't. That's why I was let go."

"Wow!" The candidate responded in amazement, leaning back in his chair with his fingers interlaced, "this might be the most exciting news I've heard all year. Do you think it will come up in the next debate?" He asked as a request for permission.

"Well, I do think that it would be a shame for you not to seize a good opportunity if you really want to win," she replied with a ruthless grin. Gary arose and leaned over his desk, with a grin, to shake her hand.

"Welcome to the team, Shana."

"That was the easiest interview I've ever had," she told herself as she settled into her new office, and she couldn't wait for Don to learn that she was working with his competition.

A knock came on the door of her apartment that evening and she opened it to see Art Jameson, the governor's top aide. She could only assume that he had been sent there by Don for damage control.

"Well, hello, Mr. Jameson," she greeted with a brisk sarcasm. "I'll bet I can guess why you're here." The lanky young man stood, smugly, in his dark suit with a look of aversion on his face.

"May I come in?" She cleared the doorway in a gesture for his entry. "Nice place," he complimented unenthusiastically with forced words, making his exasperation for her vivid. She was sure that he would have rather been anywhere else in the world than there, in her apartment, intentionally to solicit her cooperation.

"To what do I owe this pleasure?" Shana asked, offering her former co-worker a seat.

"Well, I think we both know why I'm here, so if you don't mind, I'll just cut to the chase," the arrogant visitor responded while reaching to the inside pocket of his jacket. He presented her with a folded document, intended for her signature. "The governor wants to ensure that this situation between him and you is resolved in a prompt and sophisticated manner, and he is prepared to facilitate your needs." She was appalled by his arrogant attempt to brush her off.

"Is he?" She replied with sarcasm on her lips. "That's interesting because he hasn't been willing to facilitate my needs up to this point. So basically, you're offering me hush money," Shana frigidly responded. It was clearly the governor's way of ridding himself of her, quickly and discreetly, and she was insulted by his egotism in assuming that she could be silenced so effortlessly.

"It's more of an agreement," he rationalized. "The money will ensure that your baby is more than taken care of." He spoke in a pretentious tone that she didn't appreciate.

"First of all, Art, this is our baby, Don's and mine, and, though he's pompous enough to think that he can quietly toss me aside with money, he is sadly mistaken because this child deserves its father, so you can return that envelope to him with my response. Secondly, you can relay that if he has any further messages for me, he shouldn't piss me off by sending someone else to deliver them and, lastly, you might want to inform him that I'm now working for his opponent, thanks to his failure to facilitate my needs. I have a feeling that it's going to be a very interesting election," she added with a vengeful smirk.

The novice advisor sat, stunned by Shana's revelation and dismissal of the governor's offer. Don had sent Art to her apartment on a mission that they assumed easy to accomplish. He hadn't prepared for her rebuttal, and he was left without another plan. Beads of sweat embellished his crimson face as he searched his mind for an acceptable option. "Oh, and Art, just one more thing before you go," she added condescendingly. "I will not be spoken to in that patronizing manner of yours one more time, got it?"

"We're going to have to work something out, Ms. Bradley," he uttered. "We simply can't have another scandal." He addressed her as a gullible child, which only intensified her fury.

"Well," she sighed with sarcasm, "then maybe our trusted governor shouldn't go around screwing other women outside of his marriage." It was an immense pleasure for her to put Don's young assistant in his place. When he failed to gain Shana's cooperation, he left in frustration. "Have a wonderful day, Art," she snidely bid him farewell.

At her new job the following morning, Shana reiterated to her new boss what had occurred between Art and her the previous night.

"Are you kidding?" was Gary's response. "Not only are you pregnant with the governor's child but he was bold enough to send his advisor to bribe you?"

"I couldn't believe it myself," she responded. "I sent him away with his tail between his legs."

"Unbelievable!" He exclaimed. "This just keeps getting better."

Shana spent the day helping Gary and his staff prepare for the next debate. Her previous work at the governor's office made her new job simple and she found the work to be intriguing. Unlike at Don's office, Gary employed only a few so making friends would be a challenge, she felt. Her lunch breaks were spent solo and, without Don to fill her time, her target was the only other woman in Gary's office, his aloof secretary who didn't give any indication of even wanting to know the newest employee.

Shana was ending her work day when her cell phone rang. *Donald Tatum*, the caller ID read. "This should be interesting," she thought.

"You'd better be home tonight because we need to talk," he ordered when she answered. His insistent tone sent a bittersweet blend of rage and exhilaration pulsing through her veins. She had finally claimed Don's attention, even if only for one night and under tense circumstances. It was clear to her that she was wearing him down and, perhaps, it was for that very reason that he had reconsidered the silent spell cast on her by him. It was obvious that he was displeased about her rejection of his offer but, even so, it had already brought him back to her. She couldn't deny her desire to see him again.

Shana rushed home after work to prepare the ultimate romantic atmosphere for her guest. In spite of their tribulations, she remained wildly in love with Don. He was still her goal, and her life would never be complete without him in it. His visit was her opportunity to regain her former lover's affection. After freshening up her makeup and hair, Shana chilled her finest wine, lit her most erotically scented candles and turned on a soft ballad. Her quest was clear. She paced the oak floor of her apartment until she swore a path had been tread in the grains when, at last, the knock came on the door.

"Hello," she greeted him with a seductive smile and he entered without a word. "I'm glad you came."

"What the hell are you trying to pull?" His wrath surfaced immediately.

"Well, I could ask you the same thing, Don, sending Art over here to try and buy my silence."

"You're working for my opponent!" He raged.

"You fired me, remember?" She reminded him. "I need to make a living to support our baby." She caressed the prosthetic stomach of her second suit, feeling almost like the baby was alive.

"Shana, I offered you the means to support the baby. You refused it."

"No, Don, what you offered was a bribe to keep me quiet so that you and your precious family can continue on like we don't exist," she fumed. "This baby needs a father."

"You know what this is doing to me, Shana," he pointed at her in frustration. "I can't have two families, and I won't let you blow this election!" The governor looked as if his head would explode with fury, and it was clear that she was a colossal threat to him. His mistress refused to be a hostage of his power, and the anger he displayed only reiterated her control. She held all of the cards in her hands and she was prepared to play each and every one until he agreed to her demands. Whether through intimidation, blackmail or seduction, Shana would get what she wanted. "Do you understand me?" Don glared as if he would attack her.

With a smirk of sarcasm, she peered into his icy eyes. "You're really cute when you try to take control." The young beauty made her way to the door. "You can go now."

"Shana, I mean what I say. I can destroy you!"

"You don't threaten me," she responded with a snicker. "We'll see who destroys who."

The governor lunged at her, pressing her against the wall with his hands compressed tightly on her throat while she gasped for air.

"I'm sick of you!" He yelled with a steaming face as she struggled, gasping for freedom. "You're nothing more than a common whore!" His grip on her neck constricted more tightly until she felt herself losing consciousness. She felt the very life being suffocated out of her as she fought to break free. Her legs began to buckle as she dug her fingernails forcefully into Don's face and eyes, desperate for her breath. With a knee to his groin, both of them were forced to the floor. Coughing and struggling to regain her breath, she stumbled to her bedroom, locking the door behind her with her attacker in pursuit, kicking and pounding on the wooden barrier between them as she slid her oak dresser against it.

"Open the door!" He demanded in a rage as she called the police. Her hands trembled so vigorously that just holding the phone was a challenge.

"I'm being assaulted by the governor," she announced in a shaken tone. "He is in my house and was choking me."

"Okay, ma'am, stay on the line with me. The police are en route," the dispatcher calmly responded. "Are you his wife?"

"No, I'm his pregnant girlfriend." Silence from the apparently stunned dispatcher drifted over the line.

The police arrived just minutes later to find Don on her couch with his head in his hands, exhausted and sobbing with remorse.

"Governor Tatum, sir, stand up and put your hands behind your back," one officer calmly commanded as Shana eased her way out of her bedroom.

"I'm sorry," Don tearfully remarked to his victim before being escorted to the police car.

"Are you alright, ma'am?" The other officer asked, noticing the vivid handprints on her neck.

"I'm fine," she softly replied with a refusal of medical attention. She explained to the officer what had just occurred but refused to file charges against her lover.

"I'm sorry, ma'am, but it's out of your hands. We have to arrest him."

"Please don't, sir. This will look really bad on him and, besides, I provoked the entire thing." In spite of the incident, Shana still loved Don and she didn't want to worsen the situation for either of them.

"It's out of my control," the officer explained, "but can I give you a piece of advice, between you and me?" She gave a nod and he added, "They never leave their wives. Find someone you deserve, okay?" Shana nodded with a faint smile of appreciation as the man left her apartment.

Chapter 14

Alone in the silence, she attempted to process the situation and, still, she trembled in shock from Don's violence. Shana was stunned by what had transpired and was left not knowing what to do next. Her fear had evolved into sorrow and self-pity, and she felt the need to rescue him. A sudden plague of guilt had convinced her that their altercation was entirely her fault, and she was sickened by the thought of hurting him, even as much as he had hurt her. In spite of everything that had happened between them, she loved him, unconditionally and completely. An hour later, she found herself at the jail.

"Why did you bail me out?" The shaken but calmer governor probed.

"I didn't press charges, to begin with, so it's my peace offering," Shana softly spoke as she drove him back to his car at her apartment. "In spite of what you believe, I really don't want to make things worse on you."

"My life is already shit anyway," the governor replied with a meager sigh. "I just sit and wonder how everything got so screwed up – my marriage, my reputation, the election – all of it." He stared out of the car window in self-pity. Shana listened in silence as he spoke, well aware that his blame was on her. His affair with her was at the root of his nightmare and, had he never met her, his world would have remained secure, just as he wanted it to be. She was ruining his life and the guilt of it revisited her. "He's going to win the election," Don spoke of his opponent. "Realizing that my days as governor are numbered is a jagged pill to swallow," he admitted sorrowfully. One day, you're a god and the next, you're nothing but trash." Shana parked her car next to his silver Lexus, unsure of a response to his woeful ramble in the darkened silence. After all that she had suffered because of him, Don hadn't even apologized. His concern was for himself, alone.

"How selfish of you!" She blurted, and he peered at her in disbelief. "You've tortured both your wife and me, not to mention the people of this state, whom you've also disappointed, and, now, you sit here, smug enough to feel sorry for yourself?"

The governor looked at her with the eyes of a wounded puppy, stunned by her revelation. Shana had always been his biggest supporter and he couldn't believe what he was hearing. She was supposed to empathize with him, as she had always done faithfully.

"What's wrong with you?" He responded with obscene audacity.

"Get out of the car and go home to your wife", she huffed. She'd had it with Don's self-absorbed ego.

"Oh, I see," he replied with a pompous smirk. "This is because I'm not with you. You're still sore about me staying with my family." She couldn't bear anymore of his pretentiousness.

"I said get out of the car!" His selfish attitude infuriated her, though she had to admit to herself that he was right. Even as much as his self-righteousness enraged her, Shana still craved him. She felt that nothing she did for Don was good enough. He continued to choose his wife over her and it was a dagger jabbed into her heart, time and time again. As much as she yearned to be the governor's wife one day, it was clear that she would never be anything more than his mistress, and it killed her soul. Don opened the car and turned to his pained lover.

"I'm sorry, Shana", he uttered and shut the door behind him.

The day that followed brought forth a media storm.

"Governor Don Tatum was reportedly arrested late yesterday evening," a news anchor announced on television. "Police were called to the home of a woman, claiming to be his pregnant mistress, on allegations of battery stemming from an argument between the two. Governor Tatum's attorneys confirm that he has been released on bond, pending a hearing next week."

"Oh my God!" Shana exclaimed. In the midst of the previous night's events, she hadn't even given thought to it becoming public knowledge, and she doubted that Don had either. "I can't believe this." Her only saving grace seemed to be that no one other than Gary knew her to be the governor's mistress, but it was sure to be revealed at the upcoming debate.

She imagined what Don's reaction would be when he saw the media report of his arrest. All of the recent scrutiny, coupled with this, would certainly halt his reelection campaign. He would, forever, be condemned in the public eye, and his career was essentially ruined.

"I hate this for you, Don," Shana told herself as she watched the remainder of the news report. "If you'd have just treated me better, none of this would have happened." How would he rectify the situation? She wondered. How could he explain himself and still come out of it unscathed? His only option seemed for him to confess in the eyes of ridicule.

At work that morning, Gary Dunrite appeared to prance, gleefully, into the office with an excitement that he could hardly contain and Shana knew why.

"What a fabulous morning!" He greeted his new assistant as he breezed through the room.

141

"Good morning," she uttered. "I assume you saw the news?"

"Yes, I did and you, doll, are a genius!" He presented her with a colorful bouquet. It was obvious that he assumed Shana had caused the governor's arrest, purposely, to assist Gary's triumph and, though it wasn't the case, she could only benefit from allowing him to believe it. "Sweetheart, you've just made my job effortless. Guess who's going to be the next governor?"

Shana sat at her desk with a dumbstruck smile, unable to relish her accomplishment. The guilt of what she had done to Don gnawed heavily at her and she felt suddenly empathetic toward him. The governor's entire life was in shambles. Not only was his career over but she was sure that his marriage could never endure the circumstances. Everything he had was diminishing, everything but her.

She decided to use the situation to her advantage. It was the perfect opportunity to show her lover how much she still cared for him, that she was still there, even when all else was gone. Without his career and family, Don would be needing some support, she thought. He would need to be consoled and comforted. The voicemail answered his mobile phone.

"It's me," Shana began softly. "I just wanted you to know that I'm here for you. I know we can't change anything that's happened but I'll always be here to support you. I love you, Don. Please call me."

That evening, when she still hadn't heard from him, she replayed, in her mind, the events from the previous night. The cruelty between them was callous words that could never be rescinded, and all that remained were the scars. Her heart spoke an overwhelming need to make things right between them. It pained her that the Governor hadn't returned her call, but she chose give him the benefit of the doubt. After all, she was sure that he had plenty going on, given the situation. Shana was sure that he would call her on his first opportunity away from Felicia. She poured a glass of Merlot and turned on the evening news. Details of his arrest flooded every local station on the television and radio.

"More details have surfaced in yesterday's arrest of Governor Don Tatum," the dark-haired beauty reported. "Channel 7 News has exclusively obtained the name of the woman involved in the dispute that sparked the arrest. She has been identified as Shana Bradley, former assistant to the governor, and his alleged mistress, also reportedly carrying his child."

"What?!" She squealed. Her fears had come to light as panic took control of her body. "I can't believe this!" Her heart raged violently against her chest as she picked up her cell phone to call Don again.

Within minutes, it seemed, the land line began to ring as reporters gathered outside. She was suddenly the media's top story and they wanted her input. Shana frantically turned off the ringer on her telephone and closed the blinds. On her cell phone,

143

she dialed Don's number, several times, with no response, pacing the floor of her living room in search of her next move.

"Who leaked this to the Press?" She wondered. It was painfully obvious that the police report had been sold to the news station by someone in the Sheriff's Department and there was, undoubtedly, nothing she could do about it.

"This will destroy me," she thought, sure that she would be dubbed a tramp among the town's gossiping residents, especially since Don could do no wrong in their eyes. Her face would be blanketed in shame for months to come.

The horrendous sounds of reporters pounding on the doors and windows, relentlessly calling her name, seemed to close in on her, haunting her with their echoes. Gradually, they grew louder and louder, unbearable reverberations taunting her very being. Shana fell into the fetal position in one corner, her hands in a suctioned grasp over her ears, in fear for her life as if a cavalry would soon rush in.

She was trapped within her confines with no escape from the clan of cameras surrounding her. A continuous ring of the telephone united in the deafening insanity that bullied her like demons in the night. She trembled, softly humming the tune of "Amazing Grace" in an attempt to escape it.

It wasn't until forty-five minutes later when the commotion began to calm and, still shaken, she cautiously arose to her feet. Shana was convinced that the media remained camped outside of her house and she didn't dare peek at them. In a plea for help, she dialed her boss's number on her cell phone.

"Gary, I need help," she tearfully pleaded.

"There's no way that I can get to you without going through the reporters," he responded. You're safest where you are." With no help from Gary, she called the police.

"Unfortunately, ma'am, there's nothing we can really do until they break the law," an officer explained.

"Harassment isn't breaking the law?"

"Unless one of them poses an imminent danger to you, there's nothing we can do," the officer calmly stated. "Sitting on a public road is not illegal." His words sounded preposterous to her.

After a sleepless night of strategically dodging the media in her own home, Shana felt she had no other choice but to give them what they wanted. Clad in her most intelligent-looking, navy business suit with her hair gently swept up, she cautiously emerged onto her front porch amid a deluge of camera flashes and microphones.

"Ms. Bradley, are you pregnant with Governor Tatum's baby?" One reporter openly inquired.

"Are you responsible for the governor's arrest?" Another queried.

"If I give a statement, will you all please leave my home?" She bargained in frustration. It amazed her to see a mass of microphones on a podium within minutes.

"Any time you're ready, Ms. Bradley," she heard someone say. For a moment, she stood, silent, like a scolded child too fearful to speak. The microphones were a megaphone, ready to magnify her words throughout the nation and expose her world that was once so private, making her a target for ridicule and judgment.

"I did have an ongoing affair with Governor Don Tatum during the time that I worked as his assistant." Her voice was shaken and insecure. "It wasn't intended to hurt or betray anyone, especially his family, but our relationship brought forth the child that I am carrying." Her tone grew more confident as she confessed. "There was, in fact, an altercation between Governor Tatum and myself in which he was taken into police custody and later released, but I would like his supporters, staff and the public to know that the blame is not his, alone, and that attempts are being made to resolve my differences with the governor and his family in hopes of a civil and cordial partnership in raising this child. Thank you and that's all I have to say at this time." Her words had granted her a feeling of relief. A multitude of questions crammed the air.

"How does the governor and his family feel about the pregnancy?"

"You'll have to ask him that," Shana replied. "Please, no more questions."

Though perhaps somewhat disappointed, the reporters gradually began dispersing, as promised, and she was grateful. Her statement played over and over on every news station throughout the evening, with no response from Don.

Shana pictured the media frenzy outside of the governor's mansion and she knew that he have to respond sooner than later. She replayed her words in her head, hoping that she had said everything right and apprehensively wondering what Don's explanation would be.

Chapter 15

"Even after all this time, it still doesn't seem real that you're having a baby," Carla commented as she and her friend painted the new nursery pale green.

"Especially by the governor, right?" She replied with a chuckle. She halted her job of putting together the crib and sighed a deep breath. "I guess I always envisioned the father doing this, you know? I mean, who plans it this way? I just wish he could be here."

"Why isn't he?" Carla turned to inquire. "This is his child, too, and he should be with you. You're really okay with him staying with his wife?"

"Of course not," she responded with defeat, "but he's working things out with his kids. I just need to give him that time." Carla didn't seem convinced.

Portrayed as eight months pregnant, Shana had only a few weeks left to produce a baby. She went out of state to have the baby, due to the media surrounding her, she would tell everyone but, in reality, she would be there to steal one. It wasn't something she really wanted to do, causing a new mother the painful loss of her child, but it was necessary.

The next morning, Shana turned on the news. It was a crisp, Sunday of tinted Fall leaves and brilliant sunshine, and she yearned to be outdoors but it wasn't possible with all the commotion surrounding her. Channel 7 was still airing her statement and pledging one from Don the following morning. A panel of political analysts was on a local station, discussing their predictions.

"I think that as someone in his position, holding a public office that he has been elected into, we can expect him to follow previous political protocol, apologizing for his behavior, his 'mistake, if you will, while assuring the voters that his priority remains the task at hand, being governor of this state," one opined.

"I agree, and I believe that the burden of proof will fall on the shoulders of the alleged mistress, Shana Bradley," a gray-haired suit replied. "Not only will paternity of the child need to be established, but she will have to establish herself to the public as both credible and naïve, to some extent, rather than some callous home wrecker who is out for monetary or promotional gains."

149

"All I'm out for is love," Shana commented. A few hours later, the telephone rang.

"Shana, it's Felicia Tatum calling," the stern voice said. Though she should have expected her call, it caught her by surprise.

"Well, I'm sure I know what this is about."

"Who do you think you are?" Don's wife snipped. "You think you can just step into my life and replace me? I've got news for you. You could never be me. You will never have what it takes. You think that because my husband gave you a couple lonely nights, he's actually going to leave his wife and children for you? All you were was there at that moment. You mean absolutely nothing to any of us, and that baby you're carrying probably belongs to someone else, especially since Don's had a vasectomy." Felicia's words struck Shana like a train. "A vasectomy?" She echoed to herself. Shana hadn't even given that a thought. How could she pass a baby off as his if he couldn't have any more children? Her head was spinning as she struggled for breath.

"Your argument needs to be with him, not me," she mustered up the strength to tell Felicia. "Your commitment is with him. Our relationship is really none of your business."

"It's far from a relationship, sweetheart, and yes, it is my business. I'm his wife!" She exclaimed. "You remember that. I am his wife and your so called relationship was nothing more than a meaningless fling." *Click.* She had hung up.

150

On Monday morning, Shana made her way into Gary's office, anxiously awaiting the public statement from Don.

"Well, good morning," her boss greeted. "Judging by the news, I guess I don't need to ask how it went."

"Every reporter in the state was camped outside. My neighbors must love me right now," she sarcastically spoke. "Thanks for your help, by the way."

"There was nothing I could do," he responded with a chuckle. "Turn on the television. He's about to make his much anticipated statement. I can't wait to see Tatum squirm his way out of this one."

Every news channel had reporters standing by, eagerly awaiting the governor's explanation, not only for his arrest but also for his affair. Shana could feel her hands trembling beyond control. Her stomach fluttered nervously and nausea set in as her palms grew moist.

"Why am I nervous?" She thought. She had no reason to be but anxiety had claimed control of her. She wondered what Don would say. Would he grant her her dignity or coarsely trash her name? It was naïve to assume that Don would publicly profess his love for her, especially two days before the debate, but she hoped that he wouldn't deny it either.

"Governor Don Tatum is making his way to the podium," the television reporter announced. "Let's tune in to hear his comments."

151

In his black, perfectly pressed suit, he walked slowly to the mass of microphones with a distress-ridden Felicia on his arm, whom she could see was struggling to maintain her dignity.

"Citizens of this great state of Indiana, I come to you today with a heavy heart and disappointment in myself because I have let you down as your governor. My goal has always been to serve all of you to the best of my ability. However, in light of recent events, my attention has been diverted from where it needs to be. The unfortunate truth is that I foolishly allowed myself to be misguided into a brief but intimate relationship with Ms. Bradley. My behavior was both inappropriate and unacceptable to the citizens of this state, my supporters and staff and, most of all, to my family. Therefore, after much soul-searching and tremendous heartbreak, I find it in the best interest of everyone to step down from my position and from the election."

His words left Shana with a vacancy. Don hadn't commented on his intentions with her at all but had only confessed their tryst, explaining it off as simply a fling. She had expected more from him, perhaps acknowledging the pregnancy or admitting his feelings for her. Instead, she was left with a void and plagued with disappointment. Standing by his side, it was clear to her that Felicia had every intention of staying with Don, even in spite of the public humiliation she was forced to endure.

"So, what about me?" She wondered. "Does he think this is a game, toying with my emotions and tossing me aside to move on with his boring little wife?" Shana fumed, vowing revenge on her lover for his betrayal.

"Yeah, easiest win I've ever had," Gary chuckled on his cell phone nearby. She wasn't in the mood for his hauteur. "Is this a great day or what?" He commented to her, elated about his victory. "I'm taking everyone out tonight to celebrate!" Her disappointment wouldn't permit her to share in Gary's bliss. She had more important goals.

That afternoon, when their work day was done, Gary beckoned Shana to his office and closed the door.

"Listen, Shana, I really appreciate all of your work on this campaign," he began. "It's an understatement to say that you were enormously valuable to my victory. Still, I have to be truthful and say that the road ends here."

"What do you mean? Are you firing me?" Shana was dumbfounded by his decision. It was she who had assured his win.

"I don't want to call it firing," he replied coyly. "It's simply going our separate ways. Besides, I thought it was understood that this was a temporary position during my campaign. I never promised anything more than that."

"You never insinuated that the job was temporary and you know it!" She was fuming over being used by him.

"To be candid, Shana, as governor, I simply cannot have someone with a, shall we say, tarnished reputation working with me. The people just would not approve."

"You dirty bastard!" She scowled. "How dare you, thinking you can use me like that! You think I can't sink you, too?" He stared vacantly at her with an insulting smirk.

"Please be prompt in gathering your belongings, peacefully, so that we don't have to involve security."

"You're a snake!" Shana yelled. "Everyone will know it soon!"

"I hope that you'll receive the help you need, Ms. Bradley," Gary told her as she departed.

Shana felt like her day, her life, couldn't get any worse. Nothing was going as planned, and the betrayal from both the former governor and the newly elected one seemed too much to bear. She drove home, defeated and uncertain of her plans. The day's events had altered her future, completely, and she was left not knowing what to do. At home, she dialed Don's cell phone only to hear his voicemail.

"Don, it's me, Shana," she said. "I'm so sorry for what happened and I really need to talk to you so, please, call me." She was sure he was busy with all that was going on and being forced to vacate the mansion, so she changed into a casual outfit and poured a glass of Merlot.

With a deep breath, Shana recapped her day, sulking in her desolation. She needed to figure out her next move, but much of her decision hinged on her conversation with Don. She yearned to know his intentions with her, what his future plans were and if she was part of them. Her thoughts traveled back to their intimate moments, when his caress told her that all they needed was each other. She could still feel his gaze assuring her that he loved her and his smile expressing how happy she made him. Once, he was hers, and her heart convinced her that they were meant for each other. It cried out, in desperation, to her soul mate, yearning for his love, his undying devotion. How could her feelings be so strong if it wasn't meant to be? She thought. Shana poured a second glass of wine and picked up her cell phone to check for Don's call that she already knew wasn't there.

"Why hasn't he called back yet?" She wondered and it agitated her to be put aside. "We are the topic of conversation in this country right now. We should be talking to each other." It was likely Felicia was keeping Don from calling, Shana thought. "She just can't accept us."

She glanced at the nursery of cartoon characters and white wicker, questioning if her family would ever be complete. Sitting in the rocking chair, she dreamed of cradling their baby, Shana singing soft lullabies with Don admiring from afar, with a proud smile. She was determined to have one that she could consider theirs, no matter what it took.

The third glass of Merlot had Shana's mind reeling and determined to talk to her lover. Tired of waiting for his call, she dialed his number and, again, was greeted by his voicemail.

"Why haven't you called me back?" She began. "I've been waiting for two hours now. The least you can do is return my calls!" After hanging up, Shana hadn't told him all that she had wanted to and, once again, she dialed Don's number.

"Still not answering, huh?" She said. "What's wrong, your precious Felicia won't let you speak to me anymore? Is she that insecure? I guess I can understand, given our feelings for each other. Do me a favor and tell her to get over it because I am the mother of your child and I need to talk to you immediately."

Her phone calls to Don became more frequent, nearly nonstop, for the next two hours that followed, each of them answered only by his voicemail and all of them intensifying her anger. Every call that was ignored caused her to grow more enraged with the next.

"How dare you ignore me, you spineless bastard!" Shana snapped on one of her messages. "I'm the best thing you've ever had!"

When his voicemail was full and could no longer accept messages, she began text messaging him. They, too, went unanswered, leaving her fuming. Unable to get a response from Don, Shana called his home phone.

"The number you have dialed has been disconnected," the recording informed her.

She had finished off the entire bottle of Merlot during the course of her phone calls to him, and just seeing clearly was a struggle. It didn't matter in her quest to speak to him. Shana knew she had drunk too much to drive, but her need to see Don conquered her better judgment. In her car, seeing the road was a challenge and she could feel herself swerving as she struggled to stay in the proper lane.

Finally, she reached the governor's mansion and would be able to see her lover. She could apologize for the media and reaffirm her love for him that, since their relationship had been publicized, they no longer needed to hide. Shana walked up to the front door of the mansion to see the man she adored, only to find unlit windows and a vacancy. Don and his family had moved out as quickly as they had moved in.

"Where are you?" Shana yelled while pounding on the door with her hand. It was suffocating for her to not know where he had moved to. She needed the ability to contact him, to see him and, for all she knew, Don could have left the entire state. In a panic, she dialed his cell phone number again. "How could you just leave, Don?" She asked on his voicemail, which was accepting messages again, telling her he had been checking it. "I'm standing at your door but you're gone. How long am I supposed to chase you? You need to call me immediately."

Shana, somehow, made it back to her house, safely, and made one final call to Don.

"I'm back home if you want to see me," she spoke, desolately, on his voicemail. "I don't understand why you haven't called. Maybe it's hard for you to break away. I love you and I know we can work this out." Her words were pitiful and slurred. Unable to keep her eyes open any longer, she crawled into her bed.

Shana awoke the next morning with a severe headache and Don still on her mind. Her feelings hadn't wavered from the night before and her mission to speak to him continued.

The aroma of freshly-brewed coffee scented the air as the gleaming sun peeked through the kitchen windows. She stared out at the hues of the falling foliage, strategically planning her mission. It began with a call to Don's phone.

"It's me again," Shana softly announced. "It's a gorgeous day of possibilities and I thought we could meet for coffee. Call me." She was certain that there was a legitimate reason for Don's unresponsiveness the previous night. Surely, he would be in touch with her soon, she assured herself. She turned on the news to see Gary being sworn in as the new governor.

"How could you take this from Don?" She uttered, shaking her head in disappointment. "Don deserved that position." She knew that he was devastated.

Later that morning, Shana heard a knock on the front door. She opened it to find a police officer holding some papers.

"Morning, ma'am," he greeted cordially. "I'm here to serve you with this restraining order."

"Restraining order?" She was flabbergasted that someone had placed such an order against her. "There must be some kind of mistake. Are you sure you have the correct address?"

"If you are Shana Bradley, ma'am, then yes," he responded in a manner that was matter of fact. "Have a good day."

"What is this?" Shana asked herself, fumbling to open the envelope. She scanned the document to find Don's name. He and Felicia had filed the temporary restraining order, accusing her of harassing them. She was stunned. "How could he do this?" She exclaimed. "Trying to involve a man in his child's life is harassment? I'll show you harassment!" She dialed his cell phone number, already expecting his voice mail.

"I can't believe that you would do this, Don!" She howled. "Do you really think these papers are going to keep me away? You really get off on these games, don't you? I love you and I know that you love me. That will never change, Don, no matter what papers are sent to me." I know his game, she thought. He wants me to prove my love to him. The restraining order listed his new address, which was exactly what Shana needed.

Though they were no longer camped out in her yard, the media continued to ask her for exclusive interviews, wanting her account of the scandal and the details of the affair. Their payments to her for tidbits of information were funding her comfortable lifestyle. Those she wasn't talking to appeared to be concocting tales of their own about it but all were spotlighting her in her ninth month of pregnancy. The nation was anxiously anticipating a baby, that of the former governor.

Carefully, Shana packed a diaper bag of two newborn outfits and infant supplies. On top was a nurse's uniform. Without a word to anyone other than Carla, Shana drove out of town. She was excited about her future and what the baby could bring. Once Don laid eyes on his newest child, he would never walk away again, she told herself. He was a family man who always doted on his children. Shana was sure that the baby could bring them back together. She couldn't wait to share the joy of a child with the man she loved. It would, surely, dissolve all of the problems between them.

As she began her three-hour trek from Indianapolis toward the state line to Illinois, Shana rehearsed her agenda. She had researched the Chicago hospital, thoroughly, and was confident of her plan.

The lengthy drive finally landed her at a gas station, just down the road from the lakeside hospital. After changing into her scrubs in the private exterior restroom, she drove to her destination.

"This is it," she told herself while putting on her brunette wig. Shana took a deep breath and made her way through the parking lot. "You can do this," she reassured herself in the elevator. "This is for your family. You can do it."

The elevator opened to dimly-lit passages of nursery rhyme-themed walls and the echo of a crying baby in the distance. It was a birthing center much larger than she had imagined. The pastel hallway didn't reveal any security cameras, to her relief, as she traveled confidently, following the signs to the nursery. To her surprise, no one seemed to take notice of her. The nurses, camped loyally at their station, occupied themselves with paperwork and casual conversation while some drifted from room to room, checking on their patients. Shana appeared transparent to them, almost as if she wasn't there at all.

Peering through the glass window at the newborns revealed scores to choose from. She carefully scanned each to find the one that most resembled Don. *Yates, C.* the tag read on the bassinette. The little girl was perfect. Patiently, she waited for the room to clear before going through the door like she belonged there. A nurse halted her as she wheeled the infant out the door.

"Excuse me, ma'am," she spoke and Shana's heart felt as though it had just dropped to her stomach. "You didn't sign her out," she added with a smile, handing her a clipboard.

"Oh, of course. I'm so sorry," she replied. "I just couldn't wait to see my new niece. Even rushed here straight from my shift at the hospital in Woodridge."

"I see you're a nurse, too," the woman said, easing her suspicion.

"Yeah, long hours, low pay and, yet, we render the utmost care to our patients. It's what we love, right?"

"Some days," she responded with a giggle while Shana signed a bogus name on the sign-out form.

"Well, I'd better get back to my sister before she thinks I stole her baby," she snickered jokingly. Shana discreetly ducked into a vacant and darkened room and lay the blanket-wrapped baby in the diaper bag. Casually, she descended down the elevator and out the automatic double doors without another glance from anyone.

Knowing it would be almost immediately that the nurses discovered the infant missing, Shana drove out of town as quickly as possible with the baby inside of the unzipped bag.

Just outside of town, she pulled over in an abandoned parking lot, where she secured the baby in a car seat after changing her outfit. She changed clothes and threw her wig, nurse's uniform and the infant's outfit in a nearby dumpster and headed for home. Shana was amazed by how easy it was to pull off her fete. Every part of her mission had gone flawlessly.

"You're going to complete my family, sweet girl," she said to her new daughter. "I can't wait for you to meet your daddy. He's such an amazing man and he's going to adore you."

As she drove the interstate miles, she pondered names for the baby. "Allison? That's a pretty name. Kate is really nice, too." Still, Shana wanted her to be named after Don. "How about Donna?" She asked her new daughter. "Donna Leann Tatum, after your father, Donald Lee. It's perfect." She grinned at the idea of the three of them together. Fantasies began showcasing themselves in her mind. She envisioned Don feeding Donna and rocking her to sleep. Pictures of the three of them lying in bed together danced in her head.

Halfway back to Indianapolis, Donna woke up, crying. Shana pulled into the parking lot of a fast food restaurant, where she fed her daughter and changed her diaper. It was their first connection as mother and child, and she found a warmth that she had never felt before. She was a mother nurturing her baby and it was exhilarating for her. She couldn't wait to share it with Don.

Shana arrived home and carried her new daughter into the nursery.

"This is your room," she said. "I hope you like it." She bathed Donna and put her to bed in her crib, then dialed Don's cell phone number.

"I have good news, Don," she said on his voice mail. "We have a baby girl. I hope you don't mind but I've already named her – Donna, after you. I can't wait for you to see her. She's so beautiful. I'll see you soon. Love you, darling."

The first night with Donna was virtually sleepless, forced awake to feed her every three hours. It made Shana realize just how much she needed Don's help. When he hadn't returned any of her calls at noon the next day, she became enraged.

"What kind of man won't come and see his own child?" She fumed. Immediately, she called three television stations to inform them about the baby. A single photo of Donna would earn Shana thousands of dollars in the bidding war amidst the media while ensuring that Don saw his daughter, even if only on television.

That evening, the winning network had a photographer at her house to be aired on the eleven o'clock news. Shana gave the reporter a story about going out of town, away from the media attention, to have the baby.

"Was the former governor present for the birth?" The reporter probed.

"Unfortunately, he didn't make it," she responded, clearing her throat.

"Did he sign the birth certificate?"

"I haven't had the opportunity to see him yet," she answered with the implication that he would. The interview had grown increasingly uncomfortable with each new question. "I've got a baby to take care of so the interview is over," Shana told the reporter, bluntly.

Chapter 16

Caring for an infant was new and exciting but more challenging than Shana had expected without Don's help. Doing it alone was never her plan. She was desperate for them to reunite as a family, and she couldn't understand why he wasn't returning her phone calls.

The internet buzzed with an Amber Alert that had been issued for the baby.

Unfortunately, no photo is available for baby Catherine, the article read and Shana breathed a sigh of relief. Locating the infant would be slim without a photo for the nation to see what she looked like. Shana's photo of her would be displayed on television but she thought nothing of it.

"No one will put two and two together," she told herself.

A reward of $10,000 is being offered for the infant girl's return, the story concluded.

Carla arrived, anxious for her first look at the baby.

"She's sleeping right now but come in for a peek," Shana said, leading her friend into the nursery.

"Wow, she's beautiful," Carla complimented. "Looks just like you." Shana flashed a look of confusion and pride all at the same time.

"Thanks," she responded softly, almost giggling. The two sat in the living room, sipping hot tea.

"So, what does Don think of all of this?" Carla queried.

"Truthfully, I don't know. He won't return my calls," she responded with her eyes, shamefully on the floor. "I'm sure he's still a little taken aback by it all, but it's a risk you take when you sleep with someone."

"You still don't know his plans?"

"Well, I know he loves his wife and didn't plan for this but he loves me, too, and he has an obligation to Donna as well. He has to make a decision."

"No offense, Shana, but I think he's already made it," Carla replied. "Are you prepared to raise Donna without him?"

Fury fell in Shana's eyes. "I won't have to," she scoffed. She absorbed her friend's words as demeaning. Carla was just jealous, she thought, because it was she who had all of the public's attention – and Don's. "You think you know what Don feels?" She snapped. "You only know what the media says. You weren't there to see the love that he and I shared. He loves me!"

"That's not what I'm saying," Carla rebutted.

"You've always wanted Don!" Shana barked, "and you've always been jealous of me!"

"Oh, come on, Shana. You know that's not true. I'm trying to help you," Carla responded. "Married men don't leave their wives."

"Yeah? We'll see about that." Shana was out to prove her friend wrong.

That night, Shana perched herself on the couch, close to the telephone, as she watched her brief interview on the news. She was certain that Don would be calling at any minute, after seeing his new daughter on television. When the phone rang a few minutes later, she was eager to answer it. It had to be Don, she thought.

"Hello, Ms. Bradley?" The voice on the phone was from a national magazine. "We would like to do an exclusive spread on you and your daughter."

Disappointment enveloped Shana. She yearned for the sound of Don's voice but he was slipping away, a stranger in the night. Not having him in her life was suffocating.

167

By the next morning, Shana had had enough, and she felt that something needed to be done. She was desperate for Don's attention and determined to get it. She drove to the quiet corner where his six and eight year old children awaited the school bus under a stately maple tree. The autumn morning was dark and bitter as Shannon and Joseph shivered in the icy air.

"Hi there," Shana greeted them with a grin when she pulled her car up to them, only a half block from their majestic brick house.

"Shana!" Both exclaimed, thrilled to see her. After all, she had spent a great deal of time with them while working as Don's aide. The children had missed her.

"You look like you're freezing," she said. "Let me take you to school today."

"We're supposed to ride the bus," Joseph replied with disappointment.

"Well, that's true but your dad won't mind and, besides, it's really toasty in here." Joseph and his sister glanced at each other in consideration and Shana could see their temptation. "Tell you what. I'll call your dad now and make sure it's okay," she told them and pretended to speak to Don on her cell phone. "You won't believe this but he said I could take you to breakfast before school."

"Yeah!" They roared and got into the car.

"I've missed you guys so much and I want you to meet Donna."

"Aww, hi baby," Shannon spoke to the baby in her car seat.

"You had a baby?" Joseph inquired.

"Yep, cool, huh?" Shana drove to a truck stop, on the edge of town, where they all sat down to pancakes and sausage.

"Where have you been?" Joseph probed. "My dad said you don't work with him anymore."

"That's true. I had to stop working for a little while to have Donna and spend time with her."

"Where's her daddy?" Shannon queried innocently and her words left Shana stumbling for an answer.

"Oh, um, well, he's actually away on a business trip but he'll be back home soon," she replied. It was the best answer that she could come up with on the spot.

"My mom is having a new baby," Shannon revealed, casually, and Shana nearly choked on her food.

"Really? Wow!" She stammered in a despondent attempt to disguise her resentment. "How could he betray me like this?" She thought. "How could he have another baby with Felicia?" The news devastated her.

"It's coming in May," Shannon added.

"Yeah but we don't know if it's a boy or a girl," Joseph said. Shana could feel their words suffocating her, her heart sinking more with each passing second as the rage burned her face.

"Can the two of you sit here with Donna for just one minute while I make a quick phone call?" Shana asked the children. She walked a few feet away, just out of earshot, and dialed Don's number. Just as she'd expected, his voicemail answered.

"Well, since you still don't care enough about your daughter to call me back, you've forced me to more drastic measures." Shana began. "I have Shannon and Joseph so now all three of your children are together like they should be. If you want to be part of this family, then you need to stop playing these games, Don. Perhaps now, you'll call me like you should have in the beginning. Oh, and one more thing. Don't think for one minute that Felicia's baby will take precedence over mine."

"Are we going to school now?" Shannon asked when Shana returned to the table.

"Actually, no," she responded. "We're going for a little ride."

"Where?" Joseph inquired.

"It's a surprise but I'll give you a hint in the car."

"We don't have to go to school?" Shannon asked.

"Nope, not today," Shana told her. "Where we're going is much more fun."

"Cool!" Joseph exclaimed. Shana had just loaded the children back into the car when her cell phone rang. Don's number appeared.

"Well, well," she greeted. "It took all of this for you to call me?"

"Where are my kids?" He demanded to know. She walked away from the car where they couldn't hear her talking.

"They're with me and their sister, and we're all fine," she answered calmly.

"Bring them back right now!" His voice seethed.

"I'm afraid I can't do that until Donna, your other child, gets the attention she deserves," Shana explained. "Do you think you're the one making the decisions here, because I'm the only one in that position right now. The way I see it, you will be doing what I say."

"You bitch!" He yelled.

"That's not nice, Don. Do you talk to your wife that way? Let me tell you the deal. The children and I are taking a little mini vacation for a few days to give you time to really think about what you've put me through. I'll call you periodically and, otherwise, you can speak to my voicemail the same as I had to do with you."

"I'll have you in jail before the day's out!" He threatened.

"Goodbye, love," Shana told him before turning off her phone. She couldn't be put in jail if they couldn't find her, she snickered confidently.

"Okay, kids, ready for some fun?"

"Yeah!" They exclaimed.

Shana drove an hour and a half through Indiana to a huge, indoor fun park.

"Wow!" Shannon exclaimed.

"Awesome!" Joseph chimed in.

"Didn't I tell you we were going to have fun?" Shana said.

"This is way better than school!" Joseph exclaimed with an anxious grin.

Inside, she found a table where she sat, feeding the baby while Joseph and Shannon played arcade games. Turning on her cell phone revealed numerous voice messages from Don.

"You need to return my children immediately!" His enraged voice spoke on most of them, along with further threats to have her arrested for kidnapping. Shana dialed his number, prepared for additional conflict. "I want my kids back right now, Shana!" His voice howled with fury that she knew had been building all morning.

"I don't think you're in any position to be giving me orders, Don. I'm calling the shots. Who do you think you are?" A brief silence halted the conversation.

"What do you want from me?" The wrath in his tone diluted to a sense of desperation.

"Now you ask what you can do for me", she uttered. "Well, you already know the answer to that. Your daughter needs a family. She needs two parents who love each other."

"Okay, okay," he softly surrendered with a sigh, "but Joe and Shannon don't have anything in this so please, bring them back and we'll talk about this."

"There's nothing to talk about, Don," Shana responded while waving to his children with a grin. "It's all or nothing." With that, she turned off her phone again.

After lunch and an exhausting afternoon of vacation, Shana loaded everyone into the car and headed to an upscale hotel nearby.

"Wow!" The young boy and girl said when she opened the door to their temporary abode. The reflection of a petite but luxurious, New York style apartment, the room exhibited a spacious sitting area of pinstriped sofas, colorful pillows and a large flat screen television that graced the wall. A newly shined dining table sat ornamented with gorgeous china and gold linen napkins and in a separate room, two double beds, raised high off of the ground, neatly made up with chocolates on the comforter.

"They look so fluffy," Shannon uttered in awe.

"Go see," Shana directed with a grin and the children leapt onto the beds, nibbling the truffles.

"This is so cool!" Joseph applauded.

"How about some room service?" Shana suggested.

After dinner was finished, they all traveled down to the first floor shop for some clothes and swimsuits.

"I spoke to your dad earlier today and told him how much fun you guys are having," she commented, "and he said that maybe we could stay a little longer. Isn't that great?"

"What about Mommy?" Shannon asked with troubled eyes. "She might miss us." It was obvious to Shana that the children missed their mother, but she couldn't allow a reunion until Don agreed to her terms.

"She just wants you both to have some fun, like a vacation." It was then that she realized she'd have to keep the children occupied to sway them from wanting to go home. She hoped Don would come to his senses soon.

While the young boy and girl frolicked, gleefully, in the hotel's heated indoor pool, Shana listened to numerous voice mails from their father, each demanding that his children be returned.

"If my children are not back home by eight o'clock this evening, I'll have no choice but to call the police," one of them threatened.

"Good luck finding me," she uttered spitefully. Then, she heard a hymn to her ears.

"Shana, I'm ready to give you what you want," Don's final message rang out and it was like Heaven calling her name. Her heart fluttered as she dialed his number. "Shana?" He greeted and she swore that his voice rang sweeter, more indulgent. It was a melody in her ears and a flame in her heart. She felt his love emanating from his romantic tone.

"Hi," she responded with a soft seduction. Her entire body quivered with the fire she felt for him.

"How is everything?"

"Great. The kids are swimming," she replied tenderly. "We all wish you were here."

"Well, that's what I wanted to tell you," he said. "I want to be." His words charged Shana's soul. "I'm sorry for what I've done to you. I guess I was trying to do right by Felicia, but I realize now where I need to be." Exhilaration encapsulated Shana. Finally, Don had chosen her and they could be the family she had always dreamed of. She had waited for so long but she always knew it would be.

"I'm so happy, sweetheart," she replied adoringly. "What will you do about Felicia?" Silence persevered.

"I'll talk to her tonight", he sighed. "She'll force me out immediately so I'll meet you and the kids at your house."

"Oh, um, we're actually out of town right now," she stammered, "but we can be back in the morning."

"Well, I'll come to you then." She was hesitant to reveal their location. "Shana, are you still there?" Suddenly, it seemed all too easy.

"Why the sudden change of heart?" She wondered. "Is this a trick, Don?"

"What? No, Shana. I love you and this is what I want. I can't stay with my wife just because it's the right thing to do. I know now that I have to make myself happy, the way that I am when I'm with you." With her eyes closed, Shana breathed in his symphony of sentiments. They nourished her famished soul. "Let me come and be with you, Shana."

"I'd love that, darling," she responded softly.

"I'll leave tonight," Don informed her with certainty, "and don't worry, I'll come alone."

"I'll come alone." His words buzzed in her ears over and over. "Why would he say that?" She wondered. He had gone out of his way to assure her.

It was a struggle to persuade Shannon and Joseph out of the pool with all of the fun they were having.

"Your dad is coming here in the morning," Shana announced.

"Is Mommy coming too?" The young girl asked while drying herself with the white, monogrammed towel.

"Actually, I think she has something she needs to do, but you'll see her very soon."

It was only minutes after they returned to their room that the children drifted off to sleep. Shana breathed a sigh of relief, thankfully greeting the silent relaxation after her chaotic day. After a shower, she quietly nestled into bed and dreamed of her reunion with Don. She couldn't wait to see his striking appearance, his mesmerizing eyes and breathtaking smile. She yearned for his embrace and the feel of his satin lips on hers. A fantasy of her lover arriving with flowers and a ring danced in her head as a smile graced her face.

Shana was jarred awake by the tone of her cell phone. Two hours had passed.

"Hello?"

"Shana, I'm here, at the hotel," Don said. She sprang up from her comfort and peered out the window. The darkness presented a silhouette, lit only by a night light on the side of the building next to hers. Don wasn't alone and she had suspected it. She'd sent him, purposely, to a different location to gauge his honesty, and she'd been betrayed. "What room are you in?"

"Are you alone?" It was her final test.

"Yes, of course," he answered and disappointment took control. The police officers who accompanied Don were prepared to sabotage her goal.

"We're on the fifth floor," she casually replied. "514." Shana hung up the phone and hurried the sleepy kids to her car.

"What are we doing?" Joseph queried groggily.

"We're going back home to surprise your parents," she responded and discreetly fled from the parking lot. They had made it to the highway before the next call from Don came.

"Where are you, Shana?" He probed with frustration. "You said 514."

"And you said you were alone."

"I am."

"Do you really think I'm that stupid, Don?" She snapped. I can see your band of police. Silence abounded and she imagined him examining his surroundings in search of her. "You betrayed me again and worse, played me like a fool, but the real joke is on you this time, isn't it? The real fool here is you."

"Shana, please, just let me help you," he pleaded. "This has gone too far so let's just end it now, on good terms, so no one gets in trouble." She could hear the vivid desperation in his plea.

"Well, that would be quite the fairytale ending for you but what about me? Where's my fairytale?"

"Don't do this, Shana," he begged.

"Goodbye, Don." She ended the call and began plotting her next move. Her plan hadn't gone as expected but she was determined to get her way. "He will never be mine as long as Felicia is in the picture," Shana told herself. She had come to a crossroad, left wondering which path to travel. Even with her lover's merciless words, she just couldn't give up on him. Their love was too strong, she thought, and she could never feel that way about another man. What she shared with Don was one of a kind, a once in a lifetime gift. Shana knew that walking away and going through life without him wasn't an option. She had passed the point of merely wanting to be with him. He had become her sole purpose for living. She wouldn't survive without him, she thought. He was her breath.

Chapter 17

Shana envisioned her house surrounded by police. She checked into a small motel, well outside of town, fifteen miles short of there.

"Where are we?" Joseph asked with his tired eyes only slightly opened.

"We're just stopping here to sleep for the night," Shana replied softly. "We'll see your parents in the morning. He and his sister snuggled into the double bed together and drifted, quickly, back into their slumber.

After Donna was fed and changed, she lay the infant between two pillows on the other bed to sleep. On a small notepad, she wrote, *Ran to store. Be right back* in case the kids awoke to find Shana missing. Quietly, she slipped out the door, locking it behind her. After her business was complete, she would be back for them.

The fifteen minute drive across town left her heart racing with uneasiness. Surely, the entire police department would be watching for her, she thought. Deep breaths did little to calm the nausea in her stomach as she dried her moist palms on the leg of her dark, denim jeans.

"It's for love," she assured herself. "It's for our happiness." Never before had she even dreamed of doing what she was about to embark on.

Shana parked her car in a narrow, dark alley three blocks from Don's house. Her surroundings revealed only darkened silence, bejeweled by the dimly-lit street lights lining the way. Nervous and trembling, she walked swiftly down the alley, turning to peer behind her with every couple of steps. The darkness haunted her with fears of an attacker until she found herself nearly at a jog. When she approached the block that housed her target, she saw a single police car parked at the front of the house. His car was dark and silent and Shana could see the silhouette of his head, slightly reclined back, under the faded light. It was 3:30 in the morning and she was sure that he was asleep. She scurried, discreetly, to the back of the house where the only sound was a distant bark of a dog in the neighborhood. Through a slight opening in one of the curtains was light from a lamp in the living room and Shana caught a glimpse of her rival asleep on the couch. With the back door and windows securely locked, she searched for another way in, her fingers and ears painfully chilled from the early morning frost.

At the side of the house, dense strands of ivy made their way to the eave and she noticed a trellis beneath the vines. Shana climbed up, equipped with a piece of a dead tree branch, until she reached a bedroom window. A single, swift hit shattered the pane in Joseph's room. Felicia would be on her way upstairs to investigate the noise, she thought, but she never came. She hadn't heard it.

Through the darkness, Shana continuously felt her way around Don's sanctuary, toward the sound of the television. An old movie played, in black and white, as she silently entered the room. Her rival lay, peacefully, on the couch, still in the day's outfit, with her eyes closed and hands crossed on her stomach. She looked as if she was already dead, Shana noted. Cautiously, she picked up a gold colored, satin pillow from a chair and walked slowly toward Don's wife. Shana closed her eyes, took a deep breath and pressed Felicia's face with the pillow. A fight for her breath rapidly ensued, her arms and feet flailing wildly in a desperate struggle to free herself. The attacker weighted down her nemesis in the fight to hold the pillow in place. Felicia's battle grew perilous until her movement ceased. Shana lifted the pillow with a sneer of fulfillment. A sense of exhilaration encompassed her and it was an excitement she'd never before experienced.

In the kitchen, she chose a large knife to finish Felicia off with when Don made a surprise entrance.

"What are you doing in my house?" He exclaimed, startled by her presence. "Where are my kids?" He began searching for them on his trek to the living room. "Felicia," he beckoned his wife.

"Come with me, Don," Shana urged.

"Felicia," he said, nudging his wife but she didn't move. "Felicia!"

It's no use," Shana told him.

"What have you done to her?" He demanded to know. "Felicia, wake up!" He shook her vigorously.

"I got rid of our obstacle, sweetheart," Shana responded as Don dialed 911. "I wouldn't do that," she warned.

Panic-striken, he continued, relentlessly, his attempt to revive his wife, shaking her and administering CPR.

"Don, come with me," Shana was insistent and, when he continued to ignore her, she rushed over to his wife and jammed the knife into her abdomen.

"Get off of her!" Don squealed, frantically throwing Shana off of her victim. She had been tossed across the room, into a chair.

"You're mine!" She yelled to him as he checked his wife for signs of life. The sound of sirens grew louder and the police officer who had been parked outside pounded on the front door.

"Help me!" Don called out frantically.

Shana rose up, grabbing a lamp off of a nearby table and charged her lover, striking him, violently, in the head. He screamed out in pain and fell to the floor.

"You won't deny me, Don!" She snapped.

Several police officers burst through the front door and grabbed her.

"Get off of me!" She fought to stay out of handcuffs as four of them overpowered her. "He did this," she blurted, motioning to the only partially conscious former governor.

"Kids," he stammered in a struggle to speak. "My kids." The EMTs encircled Don and Felicia.

"She's gone," Shana heard one of them say and she smirked with proud achievement.

"You're mine now," she uttered with a devious laugh.

"Where are the kids?" One officer probed but she refused him a response. "Where are the kids, Shana? Are they alive?"

"Yes," was all she said.

The officers placed Shana in the police car and she heard another say that the children had been located.

"The girl went to the motel clerk when Shana didn't come back," he said. "They've got them down at the station, along with an infant."

"Donna," Shana chimed in sadly. "The baby is Donna, from Chicago."

She sat, hopeless and defeated, in the back of the police car. Her battle had been lost. The man she loved still denied her and she was destined to be without him. Her dreams had been shattered.

A television up on the wall played as Shana sat in her jail cell the next morning.

"A tragic turn of events has unfolded in the kidnapping of the two young children of former governor, Don Tatum, and his wife," the reporter announced. "While both children, along with a newborn girl, reported missing from a Chicago hospital, have been located and are safe, we are told that Felicia Tatum was killed last night in a brutal attack by alleged mistress, Shana Bradley. Ms. Bradley has been arrested on murder and kidnapping charges, in addition to charges for an alleged attack on Don Tatum as well. He is expected to make a full recovery."

"Looks like you're going to be here a while, honey," another inmate remarked.

Nearly a year later, Shana sat on the stand at her trial, looking grievous and worn in her faded prison attire.

"Why did you do it, Ms. Bradley?" The prosecutor asked. Shana gazed adoringly at Don, who sat, nervously, before her.

"Because he said he loved me." Her eyes shed only a single tear as she peered at her former lover.

As the months passed in prison, Shana spent her time in seclusion, penning numerous letters to Don, all which were returned unopened.

"Dinnertime," she heard a baritone voice say one day as she wrote one of the letters. Looking up revealed a bronzed, dark-haired guard with a strong jaw.

"Well, hello there," she greeted with a seductive tone. "Are you married?"

www.ingramcontent.com/pod-product-compliance
Lightning Source LLC
Chambersburg PA
CBHW021008180626
46814CB00003B/1200